Dusk or Dark or Dawn or Day

ALSO BY SEANAN MCGUIRE

Every Heart a Doorway
Sparrow Hill Road

THE OCTOBER DAY SERIES
Rosemary and Rue
A Local Habitation
An Artificial Night
Late Eclipses
One Salt Sea
Ashes of Honor
Chimes at Midnight
The Winter Long
A Red-Rose Chain
Once Broken Faith

THE INCRYPTID SERIES
Discount Armageddon
Midnight Blue-Light Special
Half-Off Ragnarok
Pocket Apocalypse
Chaos Choreography

DUSK or DARK
or DAWN
or
DAY

SEANAN McGUIRE

A TOM DOHERTY ASSOCIATES BOOK

NEW YORK

DUSK OR DARK OR DAWN OR DAY

Copyright © 2017 by Seanan McGuire

Widow by Martha Keller © 1940. Used by kind permission of the author.

Cover photographs by Emma Cox/Eye Em/Getty Images (corn), and Corey Weiner/Alamy Stock Photo (New York City)
Cover design by Jamie Stafford-Hill

Edited by Lee Harris

A Tor.com Book
Published by Tom Doherty Associates
175 Fifth Avenue
New York, NY 10010

www.tor.com

Tor® is a registered trademark of
Macmillan Publishing Company, LLC.

ISBN 978-0-7653-8388-4 (ebook)
ISBN 978-0-7653-9142-1 (trade paperback)

First Edition: January 2017

For everyone who has been tempted to go,
and has found the strength to stay.
I will see you all tomorrow.

Never give their clothes away
If you want the dead to haunt you
Dusk or dark or dawn or day,
Bar no ghost from glass, they say,
If you want the dead to want you.

Leave them there by the birchwood bed,
Coat and breeches and shirt and shoes.
Fit the living or fit the dead,
Hang them up on the hooks, I said—
The hooks he used to use.

Set the table with fork and knife.
Plump the pillow and coverlid.
Where would a man who loved his wife
Lie except where he lay in life—
Same as he always did?

Leave the mirror upon the nail.
Yes, I know that the first one who
Looks in it will perceive the pale
Dead therein—and his heart will fail.
Do what I tell you to.

Set the mirror the way it was.
Let the crepe that has hid it fall.
What thing better could come to pass
Than to find my dead in the looking-glass
Hanging upon the wall?

—**Martha Keller, "Widow"**

Dusk or Dark or Dawn or Day

1

Mill Hollow, 1972

The wind howls, the rain comes down in sheets, and Patty is still dead.

The earth settles, the grave grows green with the first shoots of hungry scrub grass and dandelion root, and Patty is still dead.

The funeral bells are silent, the last of the we're-so-sorry cakes have been reduced to stale crumbs that attract marching regiments of ants, and Patty is still dead. Patty is going to be dead forever, because that's what dead *means*: dead is the change you can't take back, dead is the mistake that can't be unmade. The rain batters the tin slope of the roof until the sound of it drowns out everything else in the world—everything except for the simple, inalienable fact that Patty is *dead*, Patty is *gone*, Patty is *never coming home*. Patty died far away, in the big city where Jenna begged her not to go, the victim of the sadness that grew in her own body, in her own bones, until she picked up a knife as sharp as the end of the world.

The big-city police packed up Patty's body and shipped it back to Mill Hollow in a pine box six foot long and three foot across. Too big to hold the frail little thing Patty left behind her when she went. Too small by half to hold a girl with a smile like the morning sun and arms strong enough to hold up the world.

Thunder rumbles in the distance, low and harsh, like God clearing his throat. The walls are closing in. Jenna looks around at the curtained windows, at the muslin sheets covering the mirrors—the big one in the hall, the two smaller ones that flank the fireplace—to keep the dead from looking out. She wants to tear the fabric down, to gamble everything for the chance at seeing Patty looking at her one more time. *First person to meet a ghost's eyes is the first to die,* she thinks, and it doesn't matter, it doesn't matter, because Patty isn't here.

She rips the fabric down off the mirrors that flank the fireplace, leaves them staring blind at her, and the only face she sees is her own, skinny little Jenna, Jenna-left-behind. The absence of her sister is too much for this house to hold. *I have to run,* she thinks, and even as she thinks it, she's already running, already in motion, heading for the door without pausing to grab her coat or pull on her shoes. Ma's asleep in the kitchen, tears dried to salt-crusts on her cheeks, and Pop is God-knows-where, out in the shed or up in the attic, spending his own tears in private. He's always been a strong man, doesn't waste his time asking anyone for anything. He doesn't know how to mourn a daughter. This isn't going to be the thing that starts him looking for help.

Jenna runs alone and no one sees her go. The door slams shut behind her, closing on an empty room. The wind it makes knocks the muslin sheet covering the big hallway mirror askew. It falls by inches, fluttering slowly to the floor, leaving the glass unbarred, and everything is silent, and everything is still.

Jenna runs.

She runs across the field behind the house, heading for the forest where she and Patty used to play, her legs churning up distance and turning it into motion. The feet turn into yards behind her, and she doesn't really have a destination, and she doesn't really want one. Patty is still dead; Patty will be dead no matter how far Jenna runs, no matter how hard Jenna tries to catch up to the past. So Jenna just keeps running. She runs past the forest's edge, her bare feet squelching in the muddy soil. She runs into the dark beneath the trees. She runs, and runs, and runs until the ground crumbles beneath her heels and sends her plunging down into the ravine. She should have seen it coming; maybe she did, somewhere deep down inside. Maybe she didn't care, because she was getting what she wanted: she ran out of the world of the living entirely.

It will be two days before Jenna's body washes up on the riverbank half a mile downstream, bleached pale as bone by the currents. One of her hands will never be found. Somewhere deep in the river, fish will play hide-and-seek among her finger bones, chasing each other through the space between her thumb and index finger. Her parents will send for another long pine box, too big for her body, too small for her soul. Old lady McGeary who lives down the hollow will bring her parents a spice cake and tell them how sorry she is, and they'll be too busy grieving to see that her eyes are dry.

They'll bury her next to her sister, and everyone in the Hollow will whisper about how sad it was for the Paces to lose two daughters in the space of a season. But at least Jenna died at home, they'll say; at least Jenna died on familiar soil. Both girls will sleep better for knowing that they're resting comfortable in Mill Hollow, where the world outside will never touch them. One day, when Dan and Molly Pace follow their daughters into the dark, the whole family will be able to rest easy, together, safe at home.

Dan Pace never says anything to the people who say those things to him. Neither does his wife. They're both too busy dying by inches, sinking deeper and deeper into themselves, until the light can no longer reach them.

Jenna ran.

Maybe Jenna was the lucky one.

Maybe Jenna is still running.

2

Manhattan, 2015

"Hello?"

The voice is timid; the ones who call between midnight and three a.m. usually are. Years of socialization telling them not to bother people that late conspire to keep voices low and tones unsteady, like they're waiting for me to start yelling. I can't blame them, but it hurts my heart every time I hear it. No one should have to walk through life so afraid.

"Hi," I say, smiling warmly, letting the expression echo into my voice. Some of the people who work this shift keep mirrors taped to their monitors so they can see themselves smiling. I don't do that—I don't like mirrors—but I appreciate that they're willing to make the effort. There was a time when they wouldn't have been. "My name's Jenna." I don't ask my callers for theirs. If they want me to have them, they'll offer.

"I'm . . . I'm Vicky."

"Hi, Vicky. What's going on?"

There's a pause, brief as an indrawn breath, before she says, "I don't want to be here anymore. I'm so tired. But I don't want to go, either. I don't want to hurt people by going. How can I stay when I don't want to?"

This is a familiar question, maybe as familiar as the dance of ring and response. Not every call starts this way, but enough of them do that I don't hesitate before I say, "You can stay, even if you don't want to, by not going anywhere."

There's a shocked pause. Then she laughs, sounding almost relieved. "You say that like it's easy."

"No, I don't. I say it like it's the hardest thing in the world, because it is." Patty fought so hard, and she couldn't stay. Sometimes, even the strongest people get tired. "Do you want to tell me why you're so tired, Vicky? I'd like to listen, if you feel like talking."

They don't always. Some of them just call so they can say the forbidden words out loud: "I want to die." They mask the statement in metaphor and circuitous language, but at the end of the day, anyone who calls a Suicide Prevention Helpline is saying the same thing. "I want to die, and I don't know how to say that to anyone, and I don't know how to talk to the people who care about me without scaring them, and so I'm reaching out to strangers, because strangers are safer. Strangers don't judge, or if they do, strangers don't matter. Strangers aren't real."

I'm never going to be a person to Vicky. I'm just a voice on the other end of the phone, a temporary moment of connection in a world that has somehow knocked her off-balance, and that's what she needs right now. We talk about her hobbies. We talk about the shows she's afraid of missing, about the niece whose ninth birthday party she wants to attend this summer, about her cat, who is old and crotchety and would be lost without her.

We talk about the knives in her kitchen. She agrees to lock them in the closet for the night. Too readily: she's not a knife girl, not Vicky. I listen to the despair and weariness in her voice and I can see how she ends, strychnine in a mug of hot, sweet tea, the bitter bite of poison hidden under honey, and hope. Hope that dead will be better than alive is, because alive isn't getting her anywhere. She's a poison girl, ready to sip from the first flower that promises her oblivion.

I soften my voice, make it as gentle as I can, and ask, "Do you have someone who can keep an eye on your cleaning supplies for you?"

There's a moment of shocked silence, and I'm afraid I've gone too far. I've done that a couple of times. They can't understand how I arrow in on the methods they've been considering—and I've had to learn not to say anything when the method I pick out of their voices is too esoteric. Drowning's not common anymore. Falling's a bit more so, but it's not one of the big three: firearms, poison, or hanging. Call someone's intent as something that's not one of those and I might as well be signing their death warrants myself, because they'll hang up and never call back, and the people who need us . . .

Well, the people who need us *need* us. They can't afford to be scared away because I'm a little overzealous about my job sometimes.

To my relief, Vicky laughs again and says, "I guess I should have been expecting that. Statistically, women are more likely to go for poisons than men are. We don't like to leave a mess. We spend our whole lives learning how to be . . . how to be as neat and tidy and unobtrusive as possible, and then we go out the same way. Sometimes I think I want to make a huge mess on my way out the door. And then I think about the people who'd have to clean it up, and I'm right back to the poison. Does that make me pathetic?"

"No. It makes you human. It means you care. I don't think there's anything wrong with caring."

"I guess you wouldn't, would you?" Her voice is softer now. Contemplative. She's thinking about the conversation we've just had—and the real conversation is over now; I can hear that in her voice, just as surely as I'd heard the lure of the poisoned cup. It's all winding down and goodbyes from here. Maybe I'll hear from her again;

maybe she'll become one of my regulars, calling to update me on her progress, making sure I know she's still alive. Then again, maybe not. More than half my callers are one night only, no encores, no repeat performances.

I've met a few of them later, months or even years after they called me. I've never met any of them among the living.

"No, I wouldn't," I say. People who don't care don't choose to take the midnight shift at the Suicide Helpline. People who don't care stay home safe in their beds, or wander the nightclubs looking for something to connect them to the world, to keep them just that little bit more anchored.

"Well . . ." She takes a shaky breath, and what I hear in that sound is more reassuring than words could possibly have been. She's decided to live. Maybe not forever—maybe not even for long—but for tonight, she's decided to live. I've done some good in this world. I've paid off a fraction of my debt I owe to Patty, for not hearing the things she never said to me. "Thank you, Jenna. For listening. I . . . I really appreciate you being willing to do that."

"Any time, Vicky."

There's a click as the line disconnects. She doesn't say goodbye. I glance to the display on my computer screen: we were on that call for forty-seven minutes. Forty-seven minutes to talk a living, breathing, human woman out of killing herself. At least for tonight, Vicky will remain in the world, and that's partially because of me. I did that.

Gingerly, I remove my headset and type in the key combination that tells the system I'm done for the night. There are only a few people on the graveyard shift. Two are on calls of their own. The third is working one of the chat rooms we maintain for people who can't talk on the phone about what they're feeling, even to a stranger. His fingers dance across the keys, and I pause to admire the speed and grace with which he responds to four different conversations. I never ask to work the chats. How would I measure the time? It's too abstract. People type at different speeds; they pause and backtrack and lie so much more easily than they can when they're actually speaking to me. I'd start crediting myself with more than I deserved, and it would all be downhill from there.

Forty-seven minutes. That's what I've earned tonight. Vicky wasn't my only call, but she's the one that counts, the one where I spoke long enough, said enough of the right things, that I can legitimately say I made a difference. I hold that number as I get my coat from the closet, shrug it on, and make my way out the door, down the narrow stair to the old precode fire door that always sticks and groans when we force it open. Some of my coworkers joke about how we work in a haunted house because of that door. I always laugh with them. It's not like they're somehow on to me; Melissa McCarthy and the rest of the Ghostbusters won't be barging in with their proton packs and witty one-liners any time soon.

Which is almost a pity. The nights can get long, and we could use the entertainment.

The air outside is warm and humid, smelling of boiled hot dogs, cooling pavement, and the close-packed bodies of a million people, each with their own hidden secrets and stories to tell. There are people who don't like the smell of New York in the summer, but I find it soothing. I could stand in front of the door with my nose turned to the wind for a hundred years, and I still wouldn't breathe in everything the city has to offer. That's good. There should be some things too complex to experience, in or outside of a lifetime.

It takes me a moment to orient myself, to determine where I am in relation to Mill Hollow. The pull of it is always there, a fishhook in my heart, but sometimes it gets tangled up in the tall buildings and unfamiliar skyline, becoming twisted and strange. I follow it patiently back to the creek and the old oak by the ravine, until I know my exact position in the world again. I can read a street sign as well as anybody, but I'm always lost if I don't know where the Hollow is. That's where I'm from. That's where I died. That's what anchors me to this world. Without it,

I might as well be a sheet on the wind, blowing senseless, no more mindful than a bit of old laundry.

Everything settles into its proper place. The world makes sense again, and I start walking.

The office of the hotline where I volunteer is tucked into the back of a privately owned building in the East Village, one of those old-money havens where buying an apartment begins in the millions and climbs rapidly upward from there. The last time the top floor was sold, I think it went for five million dollars, and that was eight years ago. Most of the building is owned by a gray-haired, steel-spined old woman whose eldest son took his own life after he came home from Vietnam. She's the one who gives us our office space, free of charge, because she doesn't want what happened to her Johnny to happen to anyone else.

"He just got lost, and he couldn't see that he was already home" was what she'd said the first time we met, in the late seventies, when her hair was still shot through with black, and her eyes were still sharp without the aid of corrective lenses. She looked at me like she knew me, and when I reached for her hand to shake it, she moved politely away from me. It's been forty years. She's in her late eighties now, and she's never allowed me to touch her.

I don't think she knows why, exactly. Some people just

get a feeling when they're around me, like they shouldn't chance it. I don't push. Most of them heard something from their gran, who heard it from her gran before them, and I don't believe it's right to go crossing someone else's gran. Especially when she's right. Especially when I *am* a danger, or could be, if I wanted to.

The streets of New York are never empty. I pass a few college boys, out past when they should be studying or sleeping, a pair of tourists with no idea what they've wandered into, and pause when I see a familiar shape settled on the front steps of a brownstone. She's folded down into herself, shoulders hunched and head bowed, but Sophie has a way about her that can't be overlooked, not once you've come to see it clear.

"Sophie, what are you doing out here?" Now that I'm not on the phones, my accent is strong as moonshine and thick as summer honey. I sound like home. Sometimes I talk just to hear words the way they're supposed to sound, with their harsh edges sanded off and their tempo slowed to something that's not in such a damn hurry all the time. I crouch down, trying to catch her eye. "I thought you'd found a place."

"I didn't like it there."

"Oh." I dig a hand into my pocket, pulling out the money I was going to use for pie. I've got enough quarters to get myself a cup of coffee, and it's not like I need the calories. I put the money on the stoop next to Sophie's hip. She's younger than she looks, aged by the dirt that cakes her skin and the worries that line her face. I wish I could do more for her, and for all the others like her, but some rescues aren't mine to make. I don't touch her. I never touch her, and that hurts too, because she notices. I know that somewhere deep down, she must assume that my distance is born of the same revulsion that she gets from everyone else, the fear-born scorn that doesn't want to admit that every living human in the city is just one bad break and a few missed showers away from Sophie's stoop.

For the most part, touching the living isn't a problem for me. But when the *need* is bad enough . . . I can't risk it. Sophie's young and old at the same time, ridden hard by a world that's never been willing to take the time to be kind. She doesn't need another forty-seven minutes in this place. She needs a miracle, and the brush of my fingers would not be enough to grant it.

"Get yourself something to eat if you can, okay?" I straighten, leaving the money behind. Everyone homeless is fighting an uphill battle—for respect, for safety, for survival—but not everyone homeless is lost like Sophie. She's fallen through the cracks, and she doesn't have the tools to find her way back into the light. It's so hard for the lost. Even on the rare occasions when they have enough money for a healthy meal or a warm coat, they encounter people who won't serve them, who say a little dirt and a lot of despair are enough to sever someone from the human race.

I don't know if there's a heaven or a hell or anything beyond an earthbound afterlife full of covered looking-glasses, but if there is, I reckon some people will be getting a bit of a surprise when the time comes for their own moving on.

"Okay," mumbles Sophie, and I've done all I can do for tonight. I can't take her home, and I know from past experience that if I try to take her to the diner, she'll balk, refusing to go through the door. She has a little money, and she has her comforting shell of invisibility, which wraps around her like a cloak and protects her from the ones who might come through this night to do her harm. She's been out here a long while. It's arrogant of me to think she hasn't made her own choices along the way.

This, too, is a part of life in the city, and while each generation is happy to blame the next for the growing issues of the homeless and the disenfranchised, the fact is it's been going on since Cain was young, his brother's blood still dark and drying on his hands. People aren't so good at being good to one another. We try hard enough, but something essential was left out in the making of us, some hard little patch of stone in the fertile soil that's supposed to be our hearts. We get hung up on the bad, and we focus on it until it grows, and the whole crop is lost.

I pull my coat tighter around myself, wondering when the wind turned cold, wondering if it'll warm again before the sun comes up and the world changes yet again into something new. I walk toward the diner as quickly as I dare, mindful of the drunk tourists and college kids who sometimes stumble out of the bars, vomited into the street like so much spoiled fruit. Most of them turn and stagger back in again, determined to get as hammered as they can before last call comes and spoils all their fun. The ones that stay outside, though . . . those ones are dangerous.

The people living in this neighborhood know me. They know everyone who volunteers at the hotline. They know the work we do, and how important it is, and that we don't get paid to do it. None of them would lay a finger on me, much less knock me down and try to take my wallet out of my jacket. The frat boys and the drunks, on the other hand, have no qualms about going for a pretty young thing who doesn't have the sense not to walk alone.

I'm not what they want. They aren't what I want. I have the sense to know it; they don't. Better for all of us if I keep out of the way and keep them from learning things the hard way. Some lessons can't be unlearned.

Some lessons aren't fair to any of the parties involved, and punishing them would leave me stranded here for longer. Better to keep walking. Better to keep moving on.

The diner appears ahead of me, a skeleton of neon and bright paint glowing through the darkness like a promise, or a psalm. I pick up the pace still more, thinking of vinyl and chrome and the sweet, ever-present scent of pie crust hanging in the air, lard and sugar and flour and the memory of Ma's hands working the dough, broad and strong and weathered as the Hollow itself, with knuckles like the roots of the old elm trees. We never had the money for eating out when I was young, and even if we did, there hadn't been anyplace for us to go. Mill Hollow didn't even get a Waffle House until the end of the 1990s, much less someplace fancy like a Cracker Barrel. The diner shouldn't speak "home" to me the way that it does.

But time is on its side. Dandy's was the only thing open the night I rolled into New York City, still young and confused and convinced there'd been a mistake somewhere down the line, that one day I was going to open a door and find my sister on the other side, shaking her head and looking disapprovingly down her nose at my choices. Well, Patty wasn't waiting when I got off the bus, but Dandy's was, neon glowing through the dark. It was the first thing I saw in my new world, the lighthouse that called me home, and I'll always love it for that, no matter how much time stretches between the woman I am now and the girl that I was then.

The pie doesn't hurt.

The bell above the door chimes as I walk in. It's been making the same sound for the last forty years, fading a bit with the passage of time but always sounding clearly. The diner is only about a third of the way full. Half the people I can see are regulars, people who've been eating here for years and have learned not to comment on the things a newer patron might find strange. Like the way David caters dinners of mixed seeds and scraps for the pigeons out back, or Brenda's tendency to sit in the corner with her guitar, fingering chords and smiling, or the way I never seem to age. I *am* getting older, of course. Just slow, and steady, and not like a living girl would.

I haven't been aging like a living girl for a long, long time. Not since the night I ran out into the rain. Not since the night I died.

Brenda's in the corner with her guitar again, a cup of coffee in front of her and her guitar's neck nestled in her hand. I offer her a nod as I walk by, and she offers one back, and the compact is reaffirmed; this place is still safe. Brenda's a witch, one of the best I've ever known, all bottled magic and unforgiving judgment. She calls her power from the corn, she says, and that's why she lives in New York, where everything is concrete and glass and the only green comes from the parks and the decorative verge outside the houses. Less temptation to seize the world and do what must be done, if she's living this far from the corn.

We get along all right. I don't bother her and she doesn't bother me. She doesn't demand I take her time, and I don't run. We get by.

My seat at the counter is empty. I slide onto it, feel the vinyl conform to the curve of my buttocks, the press of my thighs. I relax a little further. Everything is normal. Everything is the way it ought to be, and I have forty-seven minutes to my credit. I lean my elbows on the counter, breathing myself into the room, and watch the ebb and flow of the people moving around me, trying to take the measure of the crowd.

There are two servers on duty tonight, Carmen and a new girl whose name I can't recall. Carmen's in her late twenties and has been working the night shift here since she graduated high school. She takes morning classes at a local college and is working her way steadily toward a sociology degree. She's happy, that's the thing. Carmen loves her job, loves her regulars, and loves the way it leaves her afternoons free to do whatever she wants to do—even if privately, I think she should spend a few more of those afternoons sleeping. She's young enough to be able to run for days on black coffee and adrenaline, and old enough to make her choices knowing what the consequences will be.

The second server is younger, the sort of stretched-thin, wide-eyed teenager that Carmen used to be. She has a baby at home, and a GED with the ink still wet tucked into her purse. She's produced it twice just to show people, for the sheer joy of being able to say, "See? See, I have a place in the world; you've tried to deny me the right to anything like it, but I got it." She'll do well here, once she finishes adjusting to the combined strain of the graveyard shift and a growing infant.

For now, though, she's dead on her feet, and she moves like every step is a chore. That decides things for me even before she drifts to a halt in front of me, opens her notebook, and asks, in a distinctly non-local drawl, "What can I get you tonight?"

Carmen would address me by name, ask how things went at the hotline, maybe have shown up with a cup of coffee already poured and piping hot in her hand. This girl could be another Carmen, given time. Or maybe she'll be something completely new, leave us for a better job and a world of prospects outside these neon-covered walls. Only one way to find out.

"Coffee," I say, with a sunny smile. "Cream and sugar, please."

She glances up from her notepad, dull surprise in her expression. Oh, she's exhausted, this one; she's near to the point of breaking, because there's never enough time. "No pie?"

"No pie," I confirm, with a shake of my head.

"Be right back," she says, and she's gone, bustling down the counter to fetch the coffeepot from the warmer.

This is the hard part. I lean farther forward, and when she fills my cup, I reach for it a little too fast, so the liquid slops over the side and onto the counter, burning my fingers. I hiss, drawing back, and she jumps in with her dishtowel and a hastily mumbled apology, trying to clean up the spill before she can get in trouble for scalding a customer, much less scalding a regular.

"I'm sorry, that was my fault," I say, reaching out as if to help. My fingertips brush the side of her hand, and just like that, I don't have forty-seven minutes owed to me anymore; I've taken them from her.

She stops cleaning for a bare moment, the clouds in her eyes clearing, replaced by a bright, enthusiastic vigor. There's no drug in this world like the feeling of a ghost touching living skin. Dead people provide a clean, natural, intensely addictive high, one that doesn't come with any downsides. We take time from the living. We leave them younger, and there ain't much humanity won't do for eternal youth.

There's a reason most of us don't advertise what we are—apart from the fact that the human race isn't quite ready for the revelation that life and living aren't one and the same. Once we're dead, there will always be those who view haunts as something other than human, and be happy to use us for what we are, instead of respecting us for what we were.

The new waitress blinks, the dazed expression leaving her face, replaced by a dreamy contentment. "I'm sorry about the coffee," she says. "How about I cut you a slice of pie to make up for it? My treat."

I've been coming here long enough to know the owners won't take the cost of that pie out of her paycheck, not when she's doing it for someone who's in as often as I am, whose habits are as predictable as mine. So I smile, and say, "That would be swell. Peach, if you've got it."

"She'll take it à la mode," says Brenda, leaning over me and plucking my coffee from the counter before I can object. "I'm paying. We'll add the price of the pie you were willing to give her to your tip."

The new girl is smart enough not to argue with Brenda, who can be a force of nature when she gets going. "Shall I bring it to your booth?" she asks.

"And the cream and sugar our little hummingbird requested, please," says Brenda. Then she's walking away, my coffee in her hand, and there's nothing I can do but follow.

Well. That's not quite true. There are a lot of things I could do, because the dead still have free will; I didn't give up being cussed stubborn when I died, thank the Lord. Not sure I could have handled being a teenage girl in the middle of a thunderstorm with no body and a whole new personality. There's only so much shock a person can handle in one day, and I think that would have been a march too far. So I could stay where I am, or I could turn around and leave the diner, or I could go all transparent and start wailing about how much I want to find my beautiful golden arm. I have choices.

I choose to follow Brenda to her booth, where my coffee is waiting and the guitar is already back in her arms, her fingers etching phantom chords along the neck. "I didn't ask for your ice cream, and I don't take any debt with it," I say, warily.

"I didn't offer any debt," she says. "There: the forms are observed. Now will you *relax*?"

I like Brenda, as much as a ghost can like a witch, as much as it's safe to drop my guard in the presence of someone like her. Forty years of sharing the same diner will do that. I sink back into the booth, feeling it mold to me same as the seat did, and shrug. "I'm here, I'm relaxed, I'm just waiting for my pie," I say. "What'd you buy it for?"

"Why didn't you have the money?" Her accent is pure Indiana, as Midwestern as the corn she says supplies her power. When she speaks, I can see a sky as endless as my Ma's knitting, and roads that cut from nowhere to everywhere, running for a horizon they know they'll never reach.

I shrug again, awkwardly this time. "Sophie was outside."

"Again?" Brenda *tsk*s. "She doesn't like the shelters. Says they make it harder to hear the city sleeping. She's right, of course, but that doesn't change the fact that she's going to wind up dead if she doesn't get things under control."

"Didn't answer the question."

"A question is a perfectly viable answer, if you look at it right," says Brenda. "I bought your pie because I saw what you did for Marisol. How much time?"

"Forty-seven minutes." There's no point lying to her. She could touch the new girl—Marisol—and know exactly how much time I'd taken. Making her go to the effort would only annoy her.

Only witches can control how much time a ghost takes. They can also force the issue. Marisol could touch me all day and not get a thing, not if I didn't want to give it. Brenda could dump a year on me in a second, if she wanted to. That's part of why they frighten me so much.

Brenda's expression softens. "How long did you work for that?"

"All night."

"There are easier ways——"

"No." I shake my head, refuting the possibility before she can lay it out in front of me. "Not for me, there aren't. I pay it back. What I take, I pay back." I'm not supposed to be here. I'm a dead girl playing at being alive, and everything I claim—whether it's a volunteer position at the crisis line or a seat on the bus—takes something from the living. I'm the damn fool who let her sister die alone in an unfamiliar city, who ran out into a storm and got herself killed. If I want to see my dying day, I'm going to earn every minute that gets me there.

"There's people who'd say the taking alone pays it back, you know," says Brenda. "You're the Fountain of Youth. Take as much as you want, they'll still come panting to you with more."

I look at her. Brenda looks back. She can be hard to read sometimes: woman has a poker face like a mountain. As always, I break first.

"You don't mean that," I say.

"You're right, I don't." She smiles. "That's why you get pie."

Then Marisol comes over with my plate, vanilla ice cream melting in rivulets down the pie crust, and sets it in front of me as ceremoniously as a knight setting the crown jewels before his queen. I reach for my fork, and Brenda smiles, and it's been a good night. A good, good night.

If I can have a million more just like it, maybe I'll have done enough. Maybe Patty will be repaid and I can finally rest.

3

Time Like a Ribbon

This is how it goes, with the dead:

When you die, the clock stops. Whatever age you are, that's the age you're set to stay, from now until forever. Not so bad, if you're one of the lucky few who die in the prime of life, happy and healthy and hale and misfortunate enough to tangle with a train or get bitten by a rattlesnake. For the rest of us, who die as children or senior citizens, when our bodies aren't equipped to do everything we ask of them, death is a new form of punishment.

What's worse, ghosts are almost always people who died too soon, shuffling off the mortal coil before their time has come—although who decides what their time should have been is something I don't know and may never learn. We know there are rules. We know we're bound to follow them, not because there are consequences for breaking them, but because they can't be broken. The world refuses to allow it. So we die too early and then we're trapped in the world, not among the living but not fully apart from them, either, until such time as we can reach the age we should have been when our hearts stopped beating.

And this, then, is the true secret of time:

Time is like water. It flows all around us, and the living can't help getting older, just like someone who walks in the rain without an umbrella can't help getting wet. But the dead, we stay dry unless we take steps to change it. Time falls right through us, and we're stuck. So how can we get older? How can we catch up to the people we should have been when we went and died?

Simple: we take the time we're missing from the living. A second, a minute, an hour at a time, wiping it off their skins and soaking it into ourselves. We can learn to control it, maybe even reverse it, but we don't have to learn how to do it. We know, right from the start. We always know.

It's a pretty good deal, for the living. They feel revital-ized when they get even a glimmer of their youth back, the clock running backward just that little amount, mak-ing everything seem right again. That's why I'm willing to do it at all. I took those forty-seven minutes from Marisol, knocking her almost an hour away from her own good death, but she'll never miss them. She'll enjoy the rush of having them gone, and if her allotted hour has moved just that much further into the future, she isn't going to complain. The living never do.

That's the problem. The dead used to walk a lot more openly among the living, making their amends and taking their allotted time from the open hands of the people who had loved them in life, the ones who would never hang a muslin sheet across the mirror's face to keep the dead at bay, or sprinkle gravedust on the mirror's frame to lure the dead inside. It used to be *safe*. But people are people, whether they're breathing or not, and no one knows who first figured out that ghosts could be used. Could be turned into a veritable fountain of youth, wicking the years away, keeping death ever further in the future. Maybe it was a wood witch, lurking in her hollow and viewing the grave as a fate she could put aside. Maybe it was a ghost, looking to make a little money for their family before they moved on. Whoever it was, they opened a can of worms that had probably been inevitable but could probably have stood to stay closed a little longer.

These days, it's not safe to be openly dead. Not because most people believe in ghosts—they don't—and not because there are a bunch of scientists with proton packs and highly paid scriptwriters stalking the corners—there aren't. Because witches are rare, but they're real, and they know that every ghost is a walking, talking pathway to the sort of American dream that's become the only one over the course of the last thirty years. Eternal youth, and all you have to do is exploit somebody's dead relatives. Witches can, and witches do, and so we hide from them as best we can, and we pray to be left alone to live our deaths until they're done.

Another thing no one knows for sure: who first prisoned a ghost in glass and learned that once we're caught between the silver and the surface, we can't control how much time we take from the living. The *living* get to control that. Worse, we can't move on, not even when we've aged past the point where we should have gone on to whatever comes next. Trap one of us and you've got yourself an answer to the question "What will I do when I get old?" You'll dump all the years you don't want on your captive dead, and they'll never be able to fight back, and they'll never be able to get away. Most witches won't go that far. They want to stay young, sure, but death comes for us all in time, and they know better than to expect the dead to be forgiving to those who've abused us.

Witches like Brenda hold on to their preferred age by bartering with ghosts to carry their years away. I've known Brenda since I stumbled into New York, and she's been comfortably settled in her late fifties for all that time, not getting any younger, but not getting any older, either. She's only asked me to take her time away once, shortly after we met, when she told me she knew what I was.

"Dead is dead, but moved on is better," she said, face serious and serene under the neon light. "Could do without six months or so, if you want it. Could be convinced to make it worth your while."

"No, you couldn't," I replied, and I told her everything. Everything. It just came pouring out in a great cathartic rush. Patty, and how she died. Me, and how I died, and woke at the back of the church during my own funeral, with Ma weeping on my bier and Pop standing there, his face empty, like a mirror with no one looking in it. How my parents covered every piece of glass in the house where I grew up, from the windows on down, so I couldn't find any purchase there, couldn't make it through the doors.

How I went looking for my sister and couldn't find her in any of the places where her spirit should have been. There wasn't even an echo. Patty was gone, just *gone,* moved on to whatever came next. She died when she was supposed to die, and I . . . I didn't, overeager little sister always following too close, always leaping before I looked. Patty went where and when and how she was supposed to go, the same way she always had. And I was the accident, just like always. Just like always.

Brenda patted my hand, the first and only time she

ever touched me, and nothing passed between us but understanding, no stolen seconds, no repurposed age. I didn't want to give, and she didn't want to take. "You've got things to work through, little girl, and I'm not going to get in the way," she said. And then she said the words that changed the world: "If you're not willing to take what you need, have you thought about doing something that would let you earn it?"

I found my first support group not a month later. I started helping people. I started *earning* the time I take, justifying it with my actions before I pull it into myself. I'm aging slowly, so slowly, but I like to think that when I finally catch up to my time—whatever age that is—and move on to wherever Patty is waiting for me, she'll be proud. She'll see I did the best I could.

She'll see how much I love her.

It's two o'clock by the time I leave the diner. The frat boys and tourists are gone, and the homeless have gone to their secret places to sleep, leaving the city for the restless and the dead. I walk with my hands in my pockets and the streetlights casting halogen halos through the fog, and I can't help thinking this is probably what Heaven will be like, warm air and cloudy skies and the feeling of absolute contentment that comes only from coffee and pie and knowing your place in the world.

At least, I hope this is what Heaven will be like. One

thing no one told me when I was first trying to adapt to existence as an earthbound spirit is that the longer I spend here, the less I want to go. I'm still working to earn my time, still fighting to get to my sister, but as the years have passed me by relatively unchanged, finding the finish line has become less and less urgent. I never want to stop helping people. The thing I used to do to make myself feel better about being a thief of time has become the thing I do because I want to. I want to make the world a better place. I want to keep people here—but among the living, not because they died too soon. I want to know that somewhere out there, somebody is living and breathing and enjoying their life because I convinced them to hold on long enough to find joy again.

I've been dead for forty years, and with every day that passes me by, I'm a little more certain I don't want to move on. This is the place I'm supposed to be. And yet I keep earning the time I need to move me closer to my dying day, because being a part of the world means letting the world be a part of me, too. I've known ghosts who stopped taking time, who decided they'd rather be haunts than people. There's nothing pretty about what happens to a spirit who decides that's the way to go. Nothing pretty at all.

New York is an expensive town, and getting more expensive with every year that passes, but the dead get by.

My landlady died in 1934, nearly fifty years before her husband. Way she always tells it, she knew he couldn't take care of himself without her, and so she came back before her family was done sitting shiva, moved right back into her kitchen, and got on with her life. She took time from her husband for years, keeping him with her, up until the day when he was hit by a crosstown bus. It was a freak accident, the sort of thing no ghost could have predicted or prevented. He had already been long past his intended dying day, and he'd had nothing to linger for—he and she had both expected that when he moved on, so would she.

Only, she still had tenants, and there was his funeral to arrange, and it seemed like she blinked and thirty years had gone by, still anchoring the neighborhood with her family-owned, rent-controlled building. "It's worth millions now," she confessed to me a few years back, both of us standing on the roof and watching the stars. Being dead means not sleeping much. "Millions! As if one little old lady needs millions more than she needs to know her people are sleeping good under roofs that don't leak, with electrical sockets that won't catch fire in the middle of the night. People think too much about money, and not enough about taking care of each other."

"They're alive."

"They won't be forever."

She was right about that. No one lives forever. Maybe that's why the living are so eager for things like million-dollar buildings and abolishing rent control: because they don't understand that they have more time than they think they do. They're swimming in the lake and I'm standing on the shore, and it's hard to understand the water when you're in it.

My locks haven't been changed since the early eighties. There hasn't been any reason to; it's not like I have anything worth stealing. I dig out my keys and let myself inside, enjoying the simple normalcy of the process. A key, a tumbler, a doorknob, the metal beneath my fingers; these are things that don't change, no matter how much time flows past me. Like me, locks remain essentially the same, updating slowly when they update at all. There's something to be said for that, especially in the here and now, where everything changes so fast. So fast. This city is not the one it was when I arrived, new ghost-girl from Kentucky, stumbling and confused. If I reside here another ten years, it will be another hundred cities before I go. That's the beauty, and the horror, of New York.

My fingers find the light switch and flick it on, illuminating my living room, the shabby furniture rescued from street corners and carted home from thrift shops and dusty secondhand stores, the bookshelves built of brick and unfinished pine. Everything is primary colors and bright patterns, like a Barbie house made large enough for me. It's the apartment I dreamt of when I was a living teenager, standing at the beginning of the seventies and believing that this, here, this playhouse paradise, this was where Patty was living; that she slept on tie-dyed sheets and opened her eyes in the morning to crystals hung on fishing wire, throwing prism patterns on poster-covered walls. Nothing else could have been good enough for my beloved elder sister. She told me all about it in her letters home, before those letters darkened into quiet complaints about how loud it was, how she never saw the stars.

Before those letters stopped.

It was years before I realized Patty was lying all along, that she was a living woman, not a dead girl, and living women need to pay their gas bills and buy food with the money they make at their dead-end, minimum-wage jobs. I could barely afford my rent back then, and I was renting from a ghost who wanted to see me settled in a comfortable haunting, not sweeping the streets like the lost spirits who wandered the alleys and parks. Patty couldn't have bought crystals by the bucket like she said, not without starving; she couldn't have made a nest of layered sheets like a fancy French pastry, not without freezing to death. She was spinning me a fairy tale of New York in the process of spinning it for herself, and when that fairy tale collapsed, it took her down with it.

The apartment is warm now. It's been years since I started paying the gas bill and installed the air conditioner, keeping the place toasty in winter and comfortably cool in summer. The reasons are scattered around the room like lumpy throw pillows, matted black and calico and tortoiseshell fur sticking up in all directions. A few stir enough to open an eye and peer in my direction, confirming my identity, but most are motionless. That's fine. They don't have much movement left in them, and there's no good reason for them to waste it on me.

Six cats, at the moment, the youngest of them fifteen years old, left behind when her owner—a friendly old man who lived down the block his whole life, dying just ahead of the sale of his building—left her for the grave. I snatched her up just before his children could consign her to the local shelter, which does its best but is overcrowded and underfunded, and doesn't have the space to keep cats that aren't likely to be adopted. Not many people want the feline senior citizens. Kittens, sure, and healthy young adults with years of purring and playing left in them. Old cats? Cats that are set in their ways and just want to be left to sleep through their twilight years, setting their own schedules, making their own rules? Old cats rarely make it to the adoption floor. People want pets that will live for years, not leave tomorrow and break their hearts on the way out the door.

But I'm already dead. I can't blame anything else for dying—and old cats aren't likely to leave ghosts behind. Old cats have already lived past the accidents that put young cats in the ground too early, and are just marking time until their destined dying days. All they need is a place to be until their hearts stop beating, and I can give them that. The local vets think I'm a saint. I think I'm just operating under special circumstances. There have been times when I've had upward of a dozen cats wandering around the apartment, meowing like creaking doors, eating their geriatric cat food and complaining about their aching bones. I've lost a few recently, which is why I'm down to six. I'll go to the shelter this weekend, see if they have anybody else in need of a home.

They always do.

One of the cats raises his head and creaks at me as I walk by. I pause to give him a pat, acknowledging that he still has a presence in the world, and he settles back to sleep. It must be nice, to be a cat.

The light from the living room filters into my bedroom, just bright enough to let me see what I'm doing. I don't need to get undressed; ghosts like stuff as much as the living do, but our clothes are a part of us, and they change when we need them to. The only thing I'm actually wearing is my jacket. I drape it over the table by the door and blink, and I'm in the nightgown I was wearing when I died, winding white cotton like a shroud, feet bare against the hardwood floor. As always, it's comfortable to put my death-clothes back on, like I'm setting the world a little closer to right. The shape of the skin under the shroud has changed as I've stolen my way into adulthood, one minute at a time, from the people around me, but this is one thing that will always fit, no matter how old I get. I was buried in it. It *knows* me.

This is the ghost of a garment, worn thin by my memory, and as gone as the rest of me. The worms have had my flesh by now. The creeping roots of trees have had the cotton stitching at my hips and the color of my hair. It's been forty years since I went to the earth, and even my bones will be crumbling by now, going down into the Hollow, like the bones of all the folk who came before me. There's something comforting in that.

It's been years since I slept in Patty's fantasy of sheets, layers surrounding and strangling me like cobwebs, like fog. When I crawl into bed, it's to settle beneath the comforting weight of my feather quilt stuffed with goose down and stitched by the hands of women I never knew. I bought it twenty years ago, the last time I went home to Mill Hollow, to see the house where I grew up. The people who live there now are strangers to me: a brother born after Patty and I were tucked in our graves, his wife, and their children. They have my family name and my mother's eyes, and they don't deserve the haunting I'd be if I got anywhere close to them. So I touched the edge of the property, and I went to visit Patty's grave, and I came home with a quilt that felt like home beneath my fingers. It wasn't much. It wasn't enough. It was everything I deserved.

I slip under the quilt, letting it weigh me down, until I feel almost like a living girl again and not an afterthought. I can feel the sunrise coming on. Ghosts walk by day same as we walk by night, but sunrise isn't our time; when the cock crows, the dead go back to their graves. Everything human needs sleep, and ghosts are still human, no matter how much our situations may have changed. We still dream.

There's no cock to crow for me here, but as the weight of several elderly cats presses the blankets down around me, I close my eyes, and I let the world drop away.

It's been years since I remembered my dreams clearly. I think I dream of flying; I think I dream of home. I know I dream of Patty laughing, Patty with butterflies in her hair, Patty before she left me to follow her dreams and her demons into a future that was never to be mine. Just like every night, I reach for her, and just like every night, she slips away.

Patty always slips away.

4

Bar No Ghost

The phone wakes me.

I open my eyes and the world is black and white. Insubstantial eyes can see, but we don't get color. Color is for the living, and for the dead whose eyes have the capacity to hold on to the light that they receive. I should probably be blind when I'm faded out like this—the laws of physics and all that—but sometimes the laws of the dead are stronger than the laws of the living.

The cats don't wake when I pass through them, my feet dangling a few inches above the floor as I drift from one room into the next. My head is still muzzy and mazed with sleep, and I don't feel like taking the effort to be solid just yet.

My answering machine was top-of-the-line when I bought it, a new, miracle invention that would make staying in touch easier than it had ever been before. Now it's an antique, clinging to life by the skin of its teeth—or the steel in its sprockets, since it's a machine. It's going to break soon, and if I can't track down another one that's simple enough for me to understand and use, early morning calls are going to get a lot more annoying. Turn solid every time someone wants to sell me insurance, or miss a lot of messages? The choice is mine, and it's an awful one.

The ringing stops. The machine beeps. And Brenda, sounding aggravated, speaks.

"I know you're there, Jenna. No way you've gone solid before noon without a damn good reason. I don't need you to answer the phone, but I do need you to listen."

Brenda has my phone number? Brenda has my phone number. I don't know how that could have happened—except I *do* know, because I haven't changed my number in years. There are dozens of people she could have asked, most of whom have no idea she's a witch, most of whom have no idea I'm dead, who wouldn't know what to do with that information if they had it. Any one of them might have thought, "Jenna and Brenda are friends," or maybe "Brenda's a sweet old lady and Jenna keeps cats; she probably wants Jenna to pet-sit or something." They wouldn't have hesitated. They wouldn't have warned me.

Brenda is still talking. "I ran Sophie down last night after you left. She said the pigeons were crying. She said, and I quote, 'There's a cat in the rafters, and no one's ever going to rest again.' So I went looking, and the ghost gang that usually hangs out down on Sixth is gone. No one's seen them in a week."

My feet hit the floor with a soft thump as I become too solid for the air to hold me. It takes a few seconds for the color to bleed back into the world, like Dorothy returning to the Technicolor fields of Oz. If I could see myself in this moment, I would look like a piece of black-and-white film flickering into existence, gaining color at the same rate as my vision, still fuzzy around the edges, like a nightmare, like a mistake. Ghosts have to sleep, and it's sleep that gets us caught, that turns us into monsters in the eyes of the people around us.

"I've been digging, and no one's seen most of the local ghosts in days. Weeks, in some cases. I'm not talking about the fringe kiddies, like that trucker who does deliveries down in the Fabric District—I mean people like Carl the Statue, and that nice boy who works at Midtown Comics. I don't know what's going on yet, but you need to watch yourself. Meet me at the din—"

The machine beeps and turns itself off, out of room to store any more words on its frayed tape. I'm solid enough now that I can reach out and press the button, triggering the message to begin playing all over again.

It doesn't make any more sense the second time. I cock my head, frowning at the speaker like that will somehow make Brenda start speaking more clearly, stop saying things I don't want to hear. The cats are waking, and a few of the bolder ones come and strop their bodies against my ankles, creaking their ancient meows as they demand breakfast. I leave the message playing and make my way to the kitchen. Brenda has my phone number. Brenda—a *witch*—knows how to find me if she wants me. That's bad enough to make me think of moving, even though there's no way I could afford anything bigger than a bottle on what I make from my day job at the coffee shop.

Brenda knows how to find me, and what she chose to do was not threaten, was not beguile: she chose to offer me a warning. That should be reassuring. It proves she's a friend, that she hasn't spent all those nights in the diner thinking about what it would be like to grab my hands and do the witchy thing, forcing me to pull the unwanted years away from her. Instead, it's just unnerving.

I spoon shreds of gravy-covered animal by-products into the dishes that line my counter, setting bowls on the floor two and three at a time, and wonder what could possibly be drawing the ghosts of my city away. Some of them are friends; some are acquaintances; some I know by rumor alone. But I've been here long enough that most, if not all, of them know me, and I like to think that if some new danger were on the horizon, at least one of them would have swung by to tell me about it.

Sophie's a street witch. That explains so much. Street witches must be common, as such things go; this day and age doesn't leave much room for farm witches like Brenda, or swamp witches like old lady McGeary who used to live down at the bottom of the Hollow. But magic adapts. Magic finds its way through the cracks in the world, and magic busts things wide open, remakes them in its own image. Pave the fields and the blacktop witches rise. Build high-rise towers to block out the sun and sky and the glass witches will climb your constructs to dance away the morning. Magic *always* finds a way.

I'd always assumed that witches took care of their own. They're solitary sorts, living their isolated lives in their specialized pockets of magic, but that doesn't mean they can't get along. Witches teach each other, share knowledge, share spells, and I've heard of witches with similar affinities sharing space. So why aren't the other street witches taking care of her? Why is she dependent on the kindness of strangers and the dead, when we don't have that much kindness to spare? The world is hard. There's no need to make it harder.

The oldest of my current crop of cats is a weather-worn old tortoiseshell whose eyes never open all the way anymore. She doesn't have the energy for alertness. She leans against my ankles as she eats her breakfast, and she either doesn't notice or doesn't care when the bare skin against her fur is covered by denim, when my daytime clothes flow into place and my winding shroud of a night-gown goes to wherever it is when I'm not wearing it. That's another nice thing about old cats: they're difficult as hell to startle.

"Keep an eye on the place while I'm gone," I say, leaning down to stroke her between her ears. The cats are fed, the day is young, and Brenda has my home phone number. It's time to talk to someone.

My apartment has two doors: the one that leads out into the hallway connected to the street, and the one at the back of the kitchen which leads to the internal stairway, intended solely for tenant use. There was a time when everyone in this building would have left their "back doors" unlocked, according to my landlady, popping in and out of each other's kitchens for a slice of cake or to borrow a cup of sugar. It was a different time. I sort of wish I'd been here to see it. It sounds a lot like living back in Mill Hollow, where for years, I didn't even know if our front door *had* a lock, much less when it would be appropriate to use it.

Every door I pass on my way up the stairs is closed and locked. Some of them are even dusty, like they haven't been opened in years. That sort of community is no longer something we reach for. That sort of community is no longer safe.

And then I reach the top of the stairs, and the door there is standing open, letting light and warmth and the sound of a radio playing hits from the 1940s into the stairwell. I poke my head inside.

Delia knocked down all the unnecessary walls years ago, leaving herself with a loft that stretches from one side of the building to the other, ceiling held up by Grecian pillars painted white and draped with artificial vines, like she's planning to stage a Shakespeare revival in the middle of her unreasonably large living room. The only distinction between kitchen and everything else is whether the floor is hardwood or large, colorful tiles. The radio is on the counter, and a large green parrot sits atop it, rocking gently back and forth in time to the music.

"Delia?" I take a step inside. Delia never leaves the door open unless she wants company; on some level, for her, this will always be the building she bought with her husband when she was young and breathing and the city was a promise she was certain would be kept. The skeleton of the place is the time, even if time has moved on around her. "You here?"

The parrot stops bobbing to whistle inquisitively at me.

"Hi, Avo. Is your owner here?" Avo—short for "Avocado"—was like my cats: a rescue. His owner had been a tenant, already old when he decided to get a "little birdie" to keep him company in his dotage. Nobody told him that parrots lived for decades. When the man had died, the bird had remained, and now lives a rent-free life with a ghost who adores him. Sometimes things work out.

"Hello, hello, hello," says Avo. "Hello, little ghostie, hello."

"Hello," I agree.

"Jenna!" The cry is glad, accompanied by the appearance of a woman who looks no more than ten years older than me. She is plump and lovely with a tangle of blonde curls, dressed in a painter's smock over blue jeans and a flannel shirt. She doesn't need the smock to protect her clothes any more than I need the jacket to keep me warm when I go outside, but sometimes the habits of camouflage can be difficult to break. "To what do I owe the pleasure? Don't tell me you thought I'd be lonely up here."

"You're never lonely, Delia," I say, submitting to a hug and a quick visual examination.

When she is done, she steps back and clucks her tongue in disapproval. "You're too thin. Have you been eating properly?"

"No." Lying to Delia has never done me any good. I don't even bother anymore. "But it wouldn't make a difference if I was. I'm dead."

"Now she tells me!" Delia throws her hands up in the

air, rolling her eyes toward the ceiling. "Dead girls don't need to eat. My life has been a waste."

A smile tugs the corner of my mouth. "You're dead too."

"Which is why I can eat whatever I want without worrying I'll get too thin and bring my own mother back from the grave to scold me for making her look like a bad parent," says Delia, matter-of-factly. "Although I tell you, Jenna-girl, if I thought a few skipped latkes might bring my dearly departed by for a visit, I would go on such a hunger strike as the world has never seen. Not a scrap would pass my lips."

The smile keeps tugging at my mouth. It's going to win soon. It always does, when Delia is around. "You know, sometimes you talk like today and sometimes you talk like yesterday. It can be sort of hard to follow."

"But when I begin talking like tomorrow, that's when you'll know there's something to be worried about, no?" Delia crosses her arms and looks at me through the tangled fringe of her hair. "What's wrong, Jenna? You're a good neighbor and a good tenant, but you don't come to see this old lady unless something is bothering you. No, don't bother arguing with me. We both know where the truth sits, and the truth says that something is not well with you."

"I don't think you get to call yourself an old lady," I

protest. "You're not that much older than I am right now."

"Whose fault is that, hmm? Those were bad boys, breaking in here like they did. They deserved to have a few extra years ladled onto them. Let *them* have my sciatica. I'll take their nimble fingers and their eyesight, and have a little more time for my art before I catch up to my dying day."

Delia has been jumping up and down the calendar since her husband died. One year she's piling on the days, taking time from people on the street like a public charity. The next, she's hunting muggers in the park, dealing out her own brand of strange vigilante justice. Because that's one of the reasons people fear hauntings, even if they've long since forgotten the details: we're not just able to take time away. We can give it back, too.

Good ghosts don't do that, unless they're people like Delia, who find a way to justify their choices under the veil of vigilante justice. She's like Batman, except instead of a cape and cowl, she has a cheery smile and a quick trip to retirement age. When she gets too old for her liking, that is. Unlike most of the dead I've known, Delia has no interest in reaching the end of her allotted span. She has her building and her tenants, and as long as New York endures, I guess so will she. There's something beautiful in that. Even among the dead, Delia will live forever.

"Okay, okay," I say, yielding to her logic before we can

get into another argument about the ethics of the way we exist. "I'm here because I'm worried. Have you heard from any other ghosts lately?"

Delia frowns. "How lately?"

"I'm not sure. Brenda called me."

"That field witch you pal around with? I don't know if anyone's told you, baby girl, but it's not good for our kind to spend too much time with theirs. They have strange ideas sometimes of the way that things should go." Delia looks briefly disturbed, her expression turning inward. Finally, she says, "They don't always play it fair."

Asking her what she means by that is as likely to trigger her showing me her latest painting as it is to get a useful answer. Treading lightly, I say, "Brenda's okay. She doesn't ask me for anything, and she buys me pie sometimes. She says the ghost gang on Sixth is missing. She says Danny from Midtown Comics is gone, too."

"Danny?" Delia scoffs. "She's wrong. Only time that boy stirs out of the city is when there's a comic book convention for him to haunt, and he always tells me before he goes. He doesn't rent from me anymore, but he knows how I worry."

"He doesn't rent from you because he's close enough to his dying day that he wanted to get rid of all his stuff. He haunts the comic book store now."

"Like I said, he knows how I worry, and he has a year

yet. More than a year, and he takes time at a rate of what? A minute a day, at best. Boy doesn't want to go. Nobody's going to make him."

"But he's not there now." Danny is like me: he's from away, although he lacks the broad vowels and mild intonations of Kentucky. He's never told anyone how he died, but he doesn't like police, and sometimes at night, I've caught him looking westward, like he thinks that somewhere out there, past the mountains and the plains and the endless rolling hills, he can find a way to see himself back home. "Have you seen any of the other tenants lately? The dead ones, I mean." We make up the bulk of the building, but there are living tenants, too. There's always at least one warm body living here.

"Not for . . ." Delia pauses before admitting, "Not for at least a week. I thought they were just too busy to visit."

"Maybe they are."

Her gaze goes distant, and I know she's doing the same thing I do after work, when I look for Mill Hollow. Only she's not looking for Mill Hollow. She's looking for her building, for the shape and the structure of it.

Her face falls. "They're gone," she says, almost wonderingly. "We're the only ghosts in this building."

"I need to go looking for the others," I say.

Delia's expression turns somber. "I'll get my coat," she says.

"Murder party, murder party!" announces Avo, following the statement with a peal of wild, distressingly human laughter.

"I'll get my coat and my parrot," amends Delia.

I sigh.

Ten minutes later, we're walking out the front door, two ghosts and a gleeful macaw. Avo rides Delia's shoulder, flapping his wings and making piratical noises whenever anyone exclaims over his presence. I hang back to keep from getting a face full of feathers, and wonder whether she knows how grateful I am to have her here.

Delia casts a smile in my direction, making sure I'm still there. She knows.

New York City by day is very different from New York by night. The city puts on her best face for the tourists, trying to lure them in, to entrap and ensnare them in her web of "everybody wants to live in New York, everybody wants to belong in the city that never sleeps." My gran used to tell us stories about goblin markets and dangerous fairy men back when Patty and I were small, and sometimes the city reminds me of those old fables. This is where you go to get lost. This is where you go to lose yourself. Maybe that's why we have the second highest population of the dead in the United States. The highest is in Las Vegas, where everything is twilight and neon and no one notices if your eyes bleed screams and your skin feels like slow murder.

New York has ghosts. Las Vegas has a haunting shaped like a city, and one day there's going to be an exorcism. Sometimes I wonder whether there's anything real under all the shadows cast by the dead.

Delia walks with purpose, and people wave to her as she strides by. The neighborhood accepts her, the way neighborhoods sometimes do; I've heard people explain her as her own daughter, even her own granddaughter, but most seem to know that she's just Delia. She's as much a part of this block as the bodega on the corner or the wonky streetlight that the city never seems to care about enough to fix, and if she ever allows herself to reach her dying day and move on, this neighborhood will be infinitely poorer for it.

"Delia?"

"Hmm?"

"Do you . . . do you know when your dying day is?" Of course she does. She's been up and down the ladder of age, and we can feel our dying days when we get close enough to them. Every ghost has a different range. Danny knew as soon as he came within a year of his—guess he was always going to die young, just not as young as he actually did—but Maria who used to hang out down by the big stone lions didn't know until she was within a week of hers. I've never felt mine calling me. I keep taking time in tiny increments, stealing whatever I think I've earned, and death remains stubbornly just outside my reach.

"Ah, Jenna, it's a beautiful day, and you're a beautiful girl, and I'm an old lady with a parrot on her shoulder and not a penny in her pocket. When did this city get so *expensive*? Time was, anyone could afford to come to New York, and that she would open her arms to welcome them in. Now she wants a credit check and a security deposit before she'll even show you to the subway." Delia shook her head. "It's not right. It's getting to where the living are so eager to eat up the world that they're not leaving any room for the dead."

"You didn't answer my question."

"That's because I was avoiding it. In my day, if a lady wanted to dodge a question, you let her. Especially if it was something that touched on her age or her home life or exactly what it was that went into her prize-winning pies."

I say nothing. I just wait. Delia likes to talk. I think that's why she was so happy to adopt Avo. Once she had him, she was no longer limited to the sound of her own voice.

Finally, she sighs, and says, "Yes, I've seen my dying day. My range seems to be a little more than a month. Scared the dickens out of me the first time I turned around and there it was, staring me in the face. So I bled off about six months, just so it wouldn't keep popping up and scaring me, and I thought about what I wanted to do."

"Didn't you want to . . ." I make a helpless gesture with my hands. "Didn't you want to go?"

"It's tempting sometimes; I won't pretend it's not," she says. "I could go. Find my Paul, and find out what he's been doing to keep busy while he waits for me. It's funny, isn't it? How we can't know when the living are supposed to go? He and I, we talked a few times about murder. About me putting a knife against his throat and cutting as gentle as I could, so he'd wake up in the same state I was in and we could be together. But we couldn't go through with it. For that, we'd have to *know* it wasn't his time, and the living don't see as clearly as we do. It could have been he was always supposed to die at my hand. Only no, he was always supposed to get pasted across an intersection because he didn't look both ways. Bastard."

"I don't—"

"So he left me here alone, and I thought, all right, that's fine, I'll start taking more time. I'll catch up to him lickety-split. But it's hard, Jenna. You'll know what I mean when you see your own dying day. We're not the living, but we're still human beings, and humans, we don't let go as easy as we should sometimes. Maybe I'll get my Paul back once I move on. Maybe I won't. 'Maybe' is a word that keeps me up at night, and it never lets go."

"Oh." We're almost to Sixth and Broadway. We should be seeing signs of the ghost gang by now. The dead know the presence of the dead. Ghosts change the landscape around themselves, not in any way permanent or prominent enough for the living to really notice, but enough that once you know what you're looking for, it's just this side of impossible to overlook.

And there's nothing. The cracks in the sidewalks are normal cracks; the leaves that fall from the hedges and domesticated trees are just leaves, falling where they will, not forming initials or strange glyphs or the abstract faces of long-dead lovers. There's no out-of-season frost in the corners of the windows, no hidden messages written in the lingering morning dew.

We are on an unhaunted corner, and that is terrifying.

Delia's face falls as she looks around, confusion giving way to bewilderment, and finally melting into fear. "Where are they?"

"I don't know," I say, and I *don't* know, and suddenly, the world is a smaller, more frightening place.

5

Don't Change Your Number

Brenda has my number but I don't have hers, and I don't know where she spends her days; I've only ever seen her at the diner, hair rimed with neon light, fingers moving on the neck of her guitar. I'll have to wait until tonight to see her, and that means waiting until after my shift at the helpline. I think, briefly, about calling in and saying I can't make it, but I can't even reach for the phone. The people who count on us to get them through the slow hours between sunset and dawn, they're not dead yet. They still have a chance to hold out until the sun comes up.

I don't mind being dead. I did, for a while, in the beginning, when I realized my life was over and that nothing I could do was ever going to bring it back, but that was a long time ago. I stopped mourning for myself when my brother was born and my parents stopped mourning for me. That seemed like long enough. That seemed like a good time to let go. But the living . . .

The living have the chance to stay that way, and they *should* stay that way for as long as possible, because life is amazing. There's so much the living can do that the dead can't. If I can keep someone alive by going to my night job, then that's what I have to do.

My day job is another matter. Delia doesn't charge her dead tenants as much as she charges her living ones—charges us just this side of nothing, in fact—but I still have to buy cat food and pay my share of the gas bill.

I make it to the coffee shop four minutes before the official start of my shift, already dressed for work, even down to the green apron with the chain logo on the pocket. We're not supposed to take those home, and technically I never do; my "real" apron is hanging in my locker, where it's been since the day it was handed to me. But spills during my shift are inevitable, and if I never wear the real thing, I never need to wash it. Ghost clothing doesn't get stained. We can always re-create it clean when the need arises.

My manager is behind the counter, steaming milk. He barely glances up as I position myself behind the register. "You're late," he says.

"Not quite," I reply.

"Time is money, you know."

I don't reply, just plaster a smile across my face and turn to wait for a paying customer. He loves that phrase, "time is money," and uses it every chance he gets. Sometimes I wish I could make him understand how wrong he is, that time is time and that's enough, because time is more precious than diamonds, more rare than pearls. Money comes and goes, but time *only* goes. Time doesn't come back for anyone, not even for the restless dead, who move it from place to place. Time is finite. Money is not.

A man walks in, tailored suit on his shoulders and caffeine craving in his eyes, and my shift begins.

It's not so bad, slinging coffee for a living. I don't mind the minimum wage; unlike my coworkers, I don't eat or go on vacation or have kids to clothe and feed. I have no college loans to pay. Sometimes I envy them those things. They get to *live*, and I got to drown while I was still in my teens. No matter how much my existence looks like living, it's not. The absence of food in my refrigerator and clothes in my closet attests to that. I work to pay the rent and keep the heat on and feed the cats, but I could stop tomorrow, and I wouldn't suffer for the change.

The customers are a steady stream, never quite overwhelming, never going away for more than a few minutes. It's soothing. I let myself sink into the rhythm of punching orders and scrawling names on cups, passing them to my manager when he's behind the counter with me, filling them myself when he's not. Some of the customers smile and drop their change in the tip jar. Others barely peel their eyes away from their phones, locked in the increasingly fast-paced race of text and response. It looks exhausting. Nothing makes me feel the age that's on my tombstone like watching people who look older than I do spending their lives staring at a screen.

My dislike of modern technology is a me thing, a lack-of-exposure thing. Danny has a smartphone, prepaid so that it didn't require a credit check, and he loves it like a child. He spends more time reading comic book news and swearing at strangers than seems strictly healthy to me, but it makes him so happy, who am I to judge?

I pause with a scoop of coffee beans lifted halfway to the grinder. Danny has a smartphone. Danny has a *phone number*.

This could change everything. I finish the drink I've been preparing on autopilot before turning to my manager and saying, "I need to take my break."

He blinks. I'm infamous among the staff of this store for never taking my legally mandated break unless forced to do so, which happens maybe twice a week, and never when there are customers in the store. I can see him struggling to come up with a reason to say "no," and so I place my left hand on my lower belly and raise my eyebrows meaningfully. He blanches.

"Go," he says, and I'm gone, walking as fast as I can toward the door that leads to the back, to the small room with its industrial-strength dishwasher and its underutilized sink. More, with its door to the break room, where a largely disused rotary phone still sits on the counter, a local-calls-only relic of a bygone age.

It's younger than I am. It will do. I put my hand on the receiver and pause, closing my eyes, to recall Danny's number.

Ghosts don't have photographic memories unless we had them while we were alive. There are things that death cannot change. But we have a flexible relationship with past and present; we can move between them to a degree, as long as we don't try to change things that have already happened. The universe is not willing to put up with that sort of thing, and smart ghosts don't mess with the universe.

The world shifts around me. I am standing on a corner with Danny, him speaking animatedly about all the features of his new phone. He is a mountain of a man with the enthusiastic heart of a little boy, and I am surprised by the wash of love that rushes over me when I see his face. It's not romantic, not sexual; it's filial. He is family, part of the congregation of the dead who treat Manhattan as their cathedral, and I don't want him to be gone unless it's because he chose to move on.

He holds up his phone, beaming, showing me the

number on the screen. "I know you'll never call me, but just in case," he says.

I snap back to the present. I dial the number, and it rings, and it rings, and there is no answer, and I know beyond the shadow of a doubt that something is very wrong; something has been broken, and I don't know why, or how, or whether or not it can be fixed. I set the phone back into the cradle and stare at the wall, willing it to give me the answers that I need.

It doesn't. It's just a wall. Eventually, my manager calls my name and I go, good little ghost, to finish out my shift, to go to the helpline, to make it to the diner. Brenda will know what to do.

She has to know.

6

Fit the Living or Fit the Dead

I only earn twenty-one minutes tonight. I have to let several calls go to my fellow volunteers when I realize I don't have the focus to take them; right now, I'd risk doing more harm than good, and that's something we can never do. We have a duty when we're on the phones, and whatever is going on in our own worlds, we owe our full attention to the people who call us for help. So I take what calls I can, and by the end of the night, I have twenty-one minutes I can honestly say the world of the living owes me.

It doesn't feel like enough. Everyone I work with has caught my discomfort, my distraction; they know I'm off my game. They don't say anything as I walk for the door, although I catch some of them watching me, concerned. We've never discussed what drives us to volunteer. I know suicide has touched us all, one way or another. We lost a volunteer a few years ago, when she could no longer resist the seemingly predestined relationship between razor and wrist. Her ghost flickered through the halls for weeks, never quite showing herself to the living, never quite daring to come inside. The others never knew they'd been haunted, but they knew something was wrong, and they're wary now. They watch each other—they watch me—in a way they never did before.

I wish I could reassure them, tell them that yes, I lost someone, but I'm not going to do anything to myself; I couldn't, even if I had felt the urge. The dead can't die. We can only move on. But truly reassuring them would require telling them what I am, and even if they believed me, they'd never look at me the same way again. Being dead and dwelling among the living comes with certain inalienable truths. "Few people like to be haunted" is one of them.

I walk quickly toward the diner, not looking for people to interact with, not reaching for connection. Tonight, connection is the last thing on my mind. That's why I don't notice Sophie before she looms up out of an alley and steps into my path, eyes wild and hands reaching for me.

"You can't *be* here," she hisses, grabbing my shoulders and clamping down, hard enough that it hurts.

I try to pull away. Her grip is too strong, and she's a witch, she's a *witch*, I can't have her touching me, I just *can't*. She's also my friend. I keep my voice level and ask, "Sophie. What's going on?"

"You can't *be* here, there are no ghosts here and you're here, so you can't *be* here." She shakes her head, not letting go. "All the ghosts of Manhattan are gone. You're alone, sweet specter, you're alone, and you shouldn't be. You shouldn't be anything."

"Let me go."

"I can't do that, can't do that, they used me, you know, they used me like a pit bull, like a pigeon seeking crumbs, seeking, seeking, Sophie in the city, the city speaks to Sophie, follow her and she'll find you what you need. I didn't know. I'm sorry. I didn't know." She grimaces, releasing my shoulders and stepping back. "There are no ghosts left here but you, Jenna, and you were always kind to me. Let me be kind to you now. Run, and don't look back. Run. This city has anchor enough without you, but your own doesn't."

"Sophie, what do you mean?" If Brenda hadn't already told me Sophie was a witch, I'd know: she's touched me without time passing between us. More, I can *see* it. The city's in her eyes, sidewalks stretching toward Chelsea, neon lights glittering like she's Broadway-bound. "Where did the other ghosts go?"

"Never give their clothes away if you want the dead to haunt you," she whispers, and turns, and runs, vanishing back into the maze of alleys. I could follow her, but I'd never catch her; she's a street witch on her home ground. The city will hide her from me out of love, and never stop to consider that maybe it should love me, too. Disturbed and distressed, I walk faster, until the diner appears, until I see Brenda through the window, her fingers moving on the neck of her guitar.

This time, I don't approach the counter, even though Marisol is on duty and smiles at the sight of me. I head straight for Brenda, sliding into the booth across from her, and demand, "What the hell is going on?"

"Hello to you, too, Jenna," says Brenda. Her fingers etch a silent chord on the strings. "I suppose you got my message."

"How did you even get my number?"

"I have my ways," says Brenda. Then she grins, and says, "You work for a chain coffee shop. I called and said I was a district manager and I needed to verify some details of your employment to avoid fining the branch. I'm pretty sure they couldn't have given me your number faster if they'd been beaming it telepathically into my mind." Her smile dies. "I know it's an invasion of your privacy. I'm sorry. I wouldn't have done it if it hadn't been so important."

"If the other ghosts hadn't been missing." It always feels a little odd to say things so baldly in the presence of the living. Never mind that most of them are paying less than no attention to the two of us, the older woman with her guitar and the gawky twentysomething who shows up every night for coffee and pie. We're just part of the background noise, and all the talk in the world of ghosts and witches and hauntings won't change that. No one believes in things like us anymore. There's freedom in that.

There's also sadness, deep and profound and undeniable. I come from a place where everyone knew everyone else, and where claiming to be a ghost in public would've had someone stopping by to have a talk with my Ma inside of the hour. It's been a long time since I lived in Mill Hollow, but some things go deeper than breath. Some things go all the way to the memory of bone. This world, where most people come and go so quickly that they never realize how slowly I age, or that Brenda doesn't age at all, this world isn't mine, and it's never going to be.

"If the other ghosts hadn't been missing," Brenda agrees. Her fingers sketch out one more silent chord on the neck of her guitar, and then, without fanfare, she sets the instrument aside. That's enough to make me sit up straighter, the hairs on the back of my neck prickling as the skin tenses. Brenda never puts her guitar down. If she hadn't told me about her connection to the corn, I would've thought that she was some sort of song witch. They're usually fiddlers, but they can bond to any stringed instrument, if they pick it up early enough.

We sit in silence for a moment, me tense and pressed against the wall of the booth, Brenda empty-handed, fingers twitching slightly, like they don't know what to do when they aren't holding the guitar. Finally, she bows her head forward, hair falling to frame her face.

"I'm the oldest witch in this city, and I should have been watching more closely," she says. Her voice is heavy with guilt. "Bill would be disappointed in me right now, and he'd be right to be. He always said I got distracted too easily, and I'd always tell him to mind his own damn business. Guess he's minding his own business now."

"Bill?" I ask—but really, I don't need to. Women Brenda's age, *witches* Brenda's age, have to come from somewhere. Something drove her out of the sweet Indiana corn, where the magic came easy and the land knew her name, all the way to the towers of Manhattan, where the only corn comes in a can, or boiled down to cloying, syrupy sweetness. Brenda's not a corn syrup woman. She's a cornhusk crone, a Corn Jenny in jeans and lumpy sweater, and this is not where she belongs.

"Bill went to the corn about a year before I came here," she says. She smiles, corner of her mouth twisting upward like an old tree root. "It was his time, and he walked in with his head held high. Said it was an easier exit than most get, going to the corn the way he did. He was a good man. We were together a long time."

First Delia, now Brenda. Everyone mourns for someone. I just died too young to do my mourning for a lover, for a spouse, for a romantic love of my life who had to go while I stayed behind—or the other way around for Delia, I suppose. Sometimes I wonder if I didn't get off light by dying when I did. It's hard to weep for what you never had.

Brenda shakes her head, smile fading back into shadow. "He was right, though. I do get distracted too easily. I get wrapped up in a single stalk and forget to watch the field. I didn't realize that the ghosts were going until the ghosts were gone."

"We're not all gone," I protest. Then I frown. "Why did you go looking?" Brenda's a witch. This could be a trap. Maybe she knows exactly why the ghosts are gone.

"Because Sophie was genuinely upset, and I wanted her to calm down enough to let me get her to a shelter for the night. It didn't work—she slept under an overpass, but I think she might be safer there. The city won't let her get hurt, and I had work to do. They're *gone*, Jenna. Not just the ones you know. The ones who keep to themselves, the ones like you, they're gone, too. Some of them have been haunting this city for centuries, and now they're nowhere to be seen."

I didn't know anyone knew all the ghosts of New York.

There's no union, no government, no central authority that tells us what to do. I know there are some support groups Uptown, masquerading as grief counseling, where the dead gather and talk about how hard it is to keep their footing in a world that insists on changing all the time. Some people say there's a vigilante in Chelsea, creeping down alleys and offloading hours onto muggers and thieves. I've always assumed that last was exaggerated, or Delia, or both. The fact remains that New York has a lot of ghosts. For all of them to be gone . . .

"How do you know?"

"City's full of glass and mirrors. I'm a witch, and you're the dead. I know."

"But we're not all gone. I'm still here. Delia's still here."

"I know." Brenda's frown deepens. "Jenna, I want you to understand that I'm not accusing you of anything. You didn't do this."

I blink. "What?"

"I had to consider it. You're still here, and so many ghosts who are older than you, more established than you, aren't. You've always been very committed to your own idea of ethical behavior. Many of them are not. You could have decided that they were a pox upon the living, and started luring them into glass. Don't look so surprised. The best ghost-hunters have always been dead themselves. No one catches a ghost like a ghost does."

My voice feels as dead as the rest of me as I struggle to whisper, "But I didn't ... I couldn't ..."

"I know." Brenda isn't frowning this time. She said those same words only a second ago, but now they're soft, gentle, like she's trying not to scare me. "You may not like how some ghosts spend their time, but you'd never interfere. You've always been willing to let others make their choices. It's part of why I respect you. That's why I know you'll tell me the truth when I ask ... Jenna, is Delia doing this? Did she decide she got to choose the afterlives of others?"

"What?" My voice is back. That's nice. It's a little too loud. Heads turn, people looking curiously in our direction before they go back to their own food and conversations.

Brenda looks at me, mouth tight, and asks, in a softer voice, "Is this your landlady?"

"No. I can't—no." I shake my head. I know she's wrong, I *know* it, but finding the words is difficult. At last, I settle on "Danny's missing too. He used to have the apartment downstairs from me. Even if Delia were doing this, she wouldn't hurt Danny. He's one of her children." She never had kids while she was alive. Her tenants—her dead ones, anyway—we're her kids. We're the ones who come over for the holidays and submit to her enthusiastic hugs, who hold her brushes when she's painting in Cen-

87

tral Park, who know how to take care of Avo when she decides she needs to go haunt her husband's grave for a week every September.

I believe Delia could hurt people. I believe anyone can hurt people. Humanity is endlessly capable of doing harm, and that doesn't change just because someone has died. But I can't believe Delia would hurt Danny.

Dimly, I realize that I've accepted that the missing dead have been harmed: they're not just off doing something interesting, distracted from the minutiae of the living by the appearance of a new haunted house or the ghost of a famous person. I died long after Marilyn moved on to whatever waits for ghosts on the other side of this world, but apparently, when she stepped out of her grave and into the light, she was greeted by a legion of adoring fans and interested onlookers. A famous ghost can pull people from hundreds of miles away, just because it's something to do.

"Delia would never hurt Danny." It's a statement of fact, small and simple and undeniable. "Sometimes she gives time back to muggers, to make a point, and I guess that hurts them. But she wouldn't hurt Danny, and she wouldn't hurt me."

"Whoever's doing this hasn't hurt you," says Brenda. "Why?"

"I don't know." I worry the skin on my left thumb between my teeth. "I don't get out much. I mostly just work and take care of the cats and try to be nice to people."

"Still, it would be possible to catch you alone. Not hard, even." Brenda glances at her guitar. "I think we need to talk to Sophie."

"Sophie never makes sense."

Brenda smiles. "You just haven't been talking to her under the right circumstances."

7

Streetwise, Shadowfoolish

We find Sophie sitting in an alley with her back against the wall, rats all around her. They spill out of her lap like eggs from a basket, and they don't flee as we approach, only lift their narrow heads and twitch their bristled whiskers and watch us come. The tilt of Sophie's head mirrors theirs. Their fur is brindled brown, and so are their tails, with patches of shockingly clean pink. I've never seen this many rats in one place.

They aren't fighting. They aren't attacking each other. A mother suckles her young in the shadow cast by Sophie's knee; two large males groom each other on Sophie's shoulder. It is a rodent Eden, and I don't understand it in the least.

Sophie's gaze sharpens, fixing on my face. "Jenna," she says. It's like hearing the town drunk sober for the first time. She smiles at my surprise. "I didn't expect to see you here. I'm sorry about the other night. I really don't like the shelters, but I appreciated the change."

"Hi, Sophie," I say. I'm confused. I glance to Brenda, who nods, encouraging me to keep talking. There's a secret here, something I'm supposed to puzzle out on my own. Turning my attention back to Sophie, I look at her again. Her eyes are bright, like the eyes of the rats around her.

Oh.

"I didn't know you were a witch until Brenda told me, and I guess that means I wasn't looking close enough; I'm sorry," I say. "I guess I didn't want to know. I don't get on so well with witches."

"Ghosts rarely do," says Sophie, her voice filled with forgiveness. "It's all right. You were always kind to me, even if you didn't know why I get confused sometimes."

The rats are watching me, eyes tracking in tandem with hers. I hold myself still, not moving away from them, and ask the next logical question: "You're not a street witch, are you?"

Sophie shakes her head. A small rat—whatever the rodent equivalent of a child is—peeks out of her hair and snuffles its nose at me. "No. I'm not."

There are all kinds of witch. People can pull power from just about anything, if they love it hard enough, if it speaks to them with enough clarity. "You're a rat witch."

"I am."

That explains why the street witches, the city witches,

the urban witches, haven't been taking care of her. No one loves the rats. They're vermin, prey for cats and dogs and city-sponsored exterminators, skittering shadows in the gutters with nowhere to belong. But they *do* have somewhere. They have wherever Sophie is, the slope of her shoulder, the shelter of her upraised knee. She is their home, and they are her eyes and ears among the city.

It makes perfect sense. It makes no sense at all.

"I can talk to pigeons too, but they don't like to come around when I'm with the nest," says Sophie. "I don't . . . do so well away from my rats. I've externalized myself for too long, and I don't reinternalize fast enough to make sense."

I glance to Brenda, who reads my confusion in my eyes, and says, "Some witches—not all, but some—can push themselves outward, into whatever their powers affect. I can go out of my body into a cornfield, if I want to. If I have reason to. Haven't done it since Bill died. There's always a risk you'll decide you like being something other than a human being, and decide to stay. The temptation was something I always felt strongly. Going out without having something to call me back seemed . . . unwise."

"I go into my rats," says Sophie. She smiles, the rats moving around her like a brown and endless tide. "They show me things I'd never see if I was all inside myself. But sometimes parts of me decide they'd rather be rats forever, and then I only get those parts back when I'm here, down in the dark, with them. Don't be sorry for me. I like this life better than the one I had before they came for me."

She doesn't give details. I don't ask for them. I spend my nights taking phone calls from the lost and the lonely, and I know all about lives that can look like purgatory, or even hell, compared to the simplicity of being down in the dark, feeling like you belong. At least Sophie found her freedom in something other than a razor's edge.

"How did you find out about the ghosts, Sophie?" asks Brenda, pulling us back on task. There's a serenity in her voice that I remember from my mother's. I glance at her, asking myself questions I never asked before. I know she was married, out in Indiana, out in the corn. Did she leave children behind when she came here to rediscover herself? She's old enough that they would have been grown, moving on to lives of their own, ready to let their mother go.

The world is full of stories, and no matter how much time we spend in it—alive or dead—there's never time to learn them all. They just go by so quickly.

"Jenna gave me her pie money," says Sophie. She casts a shy smile in my direction. "I knew what it was, and it made me want to do something nice for her, because nobody gives me their pie money. So I thought maybe one of the other ghosts would know something nice I could do. Or maybe I thought they'd give me more pie money. I didn't have my rats with me; I wasn't thinking too clearly. I just went looking. And they weren't there. They weren't anywhere. So I came here, and I asked the rats if their ghosts were missing. They said yes."

"Wait," I say. "Rats have ghosts?"

This time, the look Sophie gives me is pitying and indulgent, the look of a teacher dealing with a recalcitrant child. "Of course," she says. "Anything can leave a ghost, if it has something worth waiting for. They don't need much time to move on, though. Rats only live four years, if they're lucky. So I give them what they need, and they go where they go, and I miss them."

Sophie could be older than I am, older than Brenda, if she's constantly bleeding time off into her rats. I don't say anything. I just wait.

"There are always ghosts in the sewers, skittering and scattering and not ready to come to me and ask to go yet," says Sophie. "Sometimes they stay for years, or they wait until their loved ones are almost used up, and they take all the time from them, and let them have a little longer. But they've gone. They've all gone. I didn't realize until I saw that the human ghosts were gone, too. All the rats I talked to thought that they were coming to me, asking to move on. They weren't. They haven't. No one has asked me to hold their paw and show them the next thing in a long, long time. Months, even. They've been going without me. Or they haven't been going at all. They're just gone."

Sophie makes more sense here, surrounded by her rats, but she still doesn't follow the paths of human logic the way I would expect her to. I pause, and ask, "Are you saying they're not reaching their dying days? They're just disappearing?"

"Exactly," says Sophie.

"And the human ghosts, they're disappearing the same way," says Brenda. "They're not passing on. They're just *vanishing*. You and Delia are the last ones I know of in the city."

"You said that already." The words make me uncomfortable. They're not an accusation, not quite, but there's something unforgiving buried in them. Why do we deserve to stay when everyone else is going? Where are they going? Why?

"I'll probably say it again. Something's wrong, Jenna. You're not safe. You need to tell Delia she's not safe either. Who would take care of that damn parrot of hers if something happened to her?"

I blink. "You know about Avocado?"

"Kid, I know about everything," says Brenda, a small

smirk on her lips. She turns back to Sophie. "Did the rats see anything?"

"Yes," says Sophie, and her voice is sorrow, her voice is apology, her voice is wind blowing past my gravestone in the middle of the night. It was always going to come to this. In a world of ghosts and witches, it was always going to come to this. I was a fool for thinking it could be anything else.

Haltingly, she says, "A woman came. The rats didn't see her every time, but they saw her enough times to think that she came every time. Sometimes, they just weren't watching. A woman came, and she had a bag over her shoulder, and she approached the dead, and asked them questions, until they looked at her."

"That's when she pulled out the mirror." It isn't a question. I know how witches interact with the dead—and nothing but a witch could have come in and pulled this many ghosts away.

Sophie nods. "They were all different mirrors."

"They would have to be." Ghosts can be prisoned in any sort of glass, but if you want to hold them—if you want to keep them there long enough to get some *use* out of them—you need a mirror that holds significance for them. Best are the ones that held their reflections while they were alive. "How did she know what mirrors to use?"

"That's the first real question," says Brenda. "She must have known who they were. But some of those ghosts have been in the city for centuries. So how could a woman who doesn't live here know which mirrors to use?"

"How are you so sure she doesn't live here?"

"The rats don't know her face. More importantly, I don't know anyone who fits her description, and I know every witch and ghost in New York, New Jersey, and Connecticut. Don't look so surprised. I was a farmer before I came here. I keep track of my crops, for the sake of the fields around them."

I should probably be uncomfortable with Brenda referring to me as a "crop," but under the circumstances, it's almost comforting. It's been a while since anyone was keeping track of me. "So you're saying a witch came from out of state and stole all the ghosts?"

"I am." Brenda's voice is grim. "I have an idea of what she's going to do to them."

So do I. There's only one thing the living ever want from dead who don't belong to them: immortality. And if this witch has those ghosts prisoned in glass, she's going to get it.

8

Sleepover in Manhattan

The cats don't stir when I open the apartment door and turn on the light. I'll need to go through before bed, checking them for signs of life. It's not unusual to lose a cat every now and again, considering how old they are, and that's why I bring them back here: to give them a peaceful place to die. Even so, I don't want to deal with that tonight, and I hope they'll hold on.

"Nice place," says Brenda, stepping through the door behind me. She's looking shamelessly around, taking in my living room like a tourist taking in Times Square. She has her guitar slung over her shoulder, and a backpack she retrieved from a storage locker at a health club downtown. I'm not sure she *has* a permanent residence. I'm not sure she needs one. "How many cats do you have?"

"It varies," I say, unwilling to commit to a number before I've touched sides, felt the slow rise and fall of aged lungs and fragile rib cages. "I hope you're not allergic. I only have the couch for you, and you're going to wind up covered in cats by morning."

"I grew up on a farm, eating dirt and sexing chickens," says Brenda. "It'll take more than a little cat hair to do me in."

"Okay," I say, uncertainly. I've never had a houseguest before, not in all the time that I've been renting this apartment. I've certainly never come home with a witch. For all I know, Brenda has a mirror of her own tucked into the bottom of that bag, something come from Mill Hollow and destined to be my final resting place.

But no. She's had plenty of opportunity to ambush me, and not just tonight; stretching all the way back to the night we met, years and miles ago. She had no reason to tell me about the missing ghosts, to take me to see Sophie, if she just wanted to take me captive. I have to trust someone, and Brenda seems like the best candidate for the position. She doesn't have a mirror. She isn't here to hurt me.

"The couch is fine," she says. "I've slept on worse, and I like cats. As long as there's running water in the bathroom, I won't have any problems."

"Delia keeps the place up to code," I say. I don't bathe—going insubstantial for hours every night keeps me clean—and I only have to use the toilet if I drink coffee or eat pie, but since I do both those things just about every day, running water is important to me, too. And then there are the cats to consider. Cats require water to live.

"Good," says Brenda. She walks to the couch and plops down on the central cushion, between a geriatric calico and a black cat whose eyesight failed long before he came to me. She puts her backpack between her feet and begins stroking one of them with each hand. "I'm sorry to impose."

"No, no, it's fine," I say. If my mama could see me now, offering a guest a couch with no sheets, in a house with no food . . . "You, um. You know that once I go to bed, I won't be here anymore, right? Not for a few hours, anyway."

"I know about going to grave," says Brenda solemnly, and while I've never heard it called that before, the words are exactly right. I'm going to grave: I'm going where the good ghosts go, when they still belong here, in this world. "I'll see you in the morning, and we'll figure out what to do next."

Break a lot of mirrors; free a lot of ghosts. All we have to do is find them. "Good night," I say, and walk the floor, checking my cats before I slip into my bedroom and slip out of my skin, back into my burial shroud. Then I slip into the bed, and the world is gone, replaced by silence and the absence of time. For those few hours, I am truly dead.

What Brenda does while I'm gone is effectively a secret, because I'm not there. I have never been there. For the first few hours after I go to "sleep," there's nothing that can rouse me before my time is done.

My gone-time transitions into more ordinary slumber, and ends with sunlight slanting colorlessly through the window like beams of dusty silver, and the washed-out smell of bacon sizzling on a distant stove. Scents, like colors, are mostly stripped away by the state of being insubstantial; they haunt me, the way I normally haunt the world. I roll out of bed, set feet to the air just above the floor, and will myself toward solidity. Bit by bit, the sunlight turns golden, and the smell of bacon turns rich and fatty and nostalgic, like waking up back at home, Patty curled sleeping on her half of the bed, the morning chorus chirping and trilling in the tree outside our window. Scent is very much a part of memory, and memory is a form of time travel. It takes us back, whether or not we want to go.

Brenda is at the stove when I walk, barefoot and wrapped in my sleeping shroud, out into the front of the apartment, where the kitchen and living room flow together like water. The floor around her is a sea of cats, wolfing down their canned food with a gusto that I haven't seen from some of them in months, if ever. I give her a quizzical look.

"You died in what, the mid-seventies?" asks Brenda neutrally, flipping the sizzling bacon in the pan.

"Early," I say. "Seventy-two." That was the last year I walked the world in skin and flesh and bone; the last year the world contained my sister, pretty Patty, who should have been the one to endure, if either of us was going to.

"So you probably missed the trick," says Brenda. She begins scooping bacon from the pan to a nearby plate, where half a dozen slices are already cooling, fatty and delicious. "I'm a corn witch. I've told you that. I left Indiana because I missed Bill, and because the field was too tempting. Witches can only go out into things that have life of their own. Remember that, when whatever comes next turns taxing: a witch can never go into a ghost, or a corpse, or a bone. They can go into stones and gems and the like, but that's because the earth has a sort of life, and that's getting very metaphysical. Bacon?"

"Do I smell coffee?" I ask, in a small voice. I didn't expect to start my day with a witch waxing poetic about things that are and aren't dead. I may not sleep in the traditional way, but I'm still groggy and unsettled when I get up, and this is more than I'm equipped to handle right now.

"You do smell coffee, and pancakes," says Brenda. "Delia will be down with more eggs in a moment. She's a charming woman, your landlady. If I were twenty years younger, and she were interested in the living, I'd offer her more than a free breakfast, if you take my meaning."

"If I don't want it, can I put it down?" I ask, horrified.

Brenda laughs. "Anyway. As I was saying: witches can't go into what's dead and gone. There's no temptation for me in a can of corn. But that doesn't mean it's beyond my reach. They put corn in everything these days, thanks to the subsidies and the lobbyists. Short-sighted bastards, every damn one of them. Doesn't mean I won't take advantage."

It takes me a moment to puzzle my way through what she's saying. Then I stop, and stare at her. "Are you saying you . . . you *witched* my cats?"

"I'm saying I used the cornmeal in their food to clear up a few little medical problems they didn't need to have," says Brenda. "They'll feel better, they'll eat more, and they'll still die whenever they were meant to, because nothing I did would give them any more time. They'll just be happier until they go."

I can't be mad at her for that, no matter how uneasy I am about her using magic in my home. The cats deserve every moment of joy that they can get. "Corn witches are powerful, then, huh?"

"Why do you think we have so many lobbyists?" Brenda smiles as she turns off the stove. "Everything comes back to the soil it's planted in. Remember that."

"I'll try."

The back door bangs open, and there's Delia, Avocado on her shoulder. The parrot is shrieking about bacon-bacon-bacon; my landlady is holding a wicker basket brimming with enough eggs to feed a small army. I don't understand why until someone knocks on the front door, and Delia's face splits in a smile.

"I may have invited a few people, sweetheart. I thought you could use a little cheer before you go off chasing shadows. Everyone gets a proper wake in this house. Now be a dear, and let them in."

I can't tell her no, even though I want to: this is her building, and I'm just a tenant. So I walk to the door, my shroud wisping into my daylight clothes, and hope that whoever she's invited doesn't frighten the cats too badly.

Whoever she's invited turns out to be all the living tenants in the building. People I've never met pour into my apartment, exchanging greetings, trading names, settling in for breakfast. Some of them pet the cats. Some of them smile. All of them know Delia, who greets them like a proud parent, Avo sitting on her shoulder and gnawing on a strip of bacon. The whole scene feels familiar, eggs cooking in the pan and Brenda barking commands at anyone who wanders too close to her. One of the boys from downstairs stops by to thank me for a lovely breakfast, and I realize why this has me so on edge. It's not the strangers in my space or the fact that Brenda and Delia didn't ask me.

It's that what Delia said was accurate. This feels like a funeral. This feels like a saying goodbye. When the last dish has been washed and the last visitor slips away, I'll still be here, but my old existence will be over. I'll be someone else, someone who works with witches instead of avoiding them, someone who looks for missing people instead of staying safe behind a phone and helping the lost find their own way home.

My first funeral was no fun. This one isn't much better.

It takes a little over an hour for the occupants of my building to devour everything Brenda has cooked, everything Delia has provided. Then they stream out, some pausing to pet the cats, vanishing back into the halls and the safety of their own homes. I feel a pang of loss. I'll likely never see most of them again. The fact that I've never seen most of them before doesn't matter. They became a part of my world when they came to breakfast in my living room, and now I have something I can grieve for.

I should have made an effort. I should have met them before this. I should have *lived*.

The door closes behind the last guest. The only sound is Avo crunching on a piece of toast. The parrot has eaten enough to make up for the fact that I haven't eaten anything at all, too nervous to stomach anything but air. I look to Brenda, and I wait.

"I don't know where the other ghosts went," says Brenda. "I know they were taken. I know someone out there is barring ghosts in glass. And I know Delia has to stay here."

"I provide housing for more than just ghosts," says Delia. She looks uncomfortable, like the words are bitter in her mouth. "There's families, college students, people who'd be priced right out of what this city has turned into, if they didn't have me to keep a roof over their heads."

"What she's not saying is that right now, she's the senior ghost in Manhattan," says Brenda. "That comes with certain responsibilities. One of them is staying here, in case new ghosts come along and need to be taught the rules of the city."

"Delia's always been good at doing that," I say numbly.

"It was always just helping out in an unofficial capacity before," says Delia. "Hopefully, it will be again soon, when those other ghosts come back. I don't want to be in charge of anything. Being in charge of things will interfere with my painting something fierce."

I laugh. I can't help it.

The phone rings.

We all turn toward it. I'm the first to find my voice. "No

one from the hotline would be calling me at this hour, and today's my day off from work," I say. "No one should be calling me at all." Because that's the real tragedy of being a dead girl in a world filled with the living: no one calls. No one comes over for breakfast. I am a tourist here, in a place where I never belonged, and there are very few people who would miss me if I were gone.

"Aren't you going to see who it is?" asks Delia, when the ringing gets to be too much.

I pick up the receiver. It's cold and heavy in my hand. "Hello?"

"Jenna!" Danny sounds so relieved to hear my voice that it hurts. I almost drop the phone. "I was afraid you wouldn't pick up."

"Danny?" Brenda stiffens. Delia looks relieved. I try to focus on the sound of his voice. "Danny, where *are* you? We're all worried sick. The ghosts are gone. All the ghosts are gone."

"That's why I'm hiding—because someone's been stealing ghosts, and I don't want to be next," says Danny. "I was calling to make sure *you* were okay. Where are you, Jenna? Are you being safe? Are you being careful?"

"I'm at home," I say, frowning. "You called me. You should know that. How did you get this number?" A lot of people who shouldn't have my number have been calling me lately. It's starting to get on my nerves.

"I—" Danny stops after that one syllable, leaving it hanging for several seconds before he says, "Just be careful. Stay in public places, if you can. Don't go to the helpline. It's too predictable. Try the park, or Times Square, someplace where no one can get you alone. I'll do my best to call again."

The line goes dead. I lower the receiver, frowning. "I never gave him my number," I say. "How can he call me if he doesn't have my number?"

"There are many kinds of witches," says Brenda. Then, without giving me a chance to stop and think, she asks, "Where did the call originate?"

"Mill Hollow, Kentucky," I say, with equal speed. Then I stop, blinking slowly, and turn to stare at her. "How did you . . . how did *I* . . ."

"Ghosts can always find home, and there had to be a reason you'd been left alone this long," says Brenda. She looks to Delia. "Lock your doors and windows tight. It's not safe here anymore. I know you can't leave—"

"You know I *won't* leave," says Delia firmly.

Brenda smiles. "You won't leave. Yes. But you need to stay secure, if you can. We don't want Manhattan to come unmoored."

Delia sobers. "No," she agrees. "We don't want that."

I look between the two of them, and I have no idea what they're talking about. If I'd lived—if I'd grown up and grown older as a living human girl—I'd be an adult by now. As it stands, in some ways, I'm still a child. I always will be, right up until I reach my dying day and step across the line into whatever waits for ghosts who have moved on. It's frustrating under the best of circumstances. Right now, it's terrifying.

"What does 'unmoored' mean?" I ask.

Both older women stop, turning to face me. Delia's mouth works like she's trying to speak but can't find the words. That just makes things worse. Brenda can be silent. I've seen it, seen her sitting comfortable at the diner counter with a cup of coffee in her hand, letting the world move around her like a promise. But Delia doesn't hold her peace. "I'm not resting in it, so I don't see the need to cling to it" was what she told me once, when I asked if talking all the time got as exhausting for her as it was for me. Delia is never silent, and now Delia can't make a sound.

This is where I should turn and run. This is where I should go see California, catch a plane to Hawaii, anything to get me away from this suddenly unsafe apartment full of ancient cats and silent ghosts, anything to take myself out of the line of fire. I'm Jenna, I'm the girl who runs. I ran from Patty's death and into the storm that killed me. I ran from Mill Hollow and the slow acidic ache of watching my parents age and die while I stood outside of time, exiled by my own actions. Ghosts are going missing, Danny is calling me from Mill Hollow, and Delia has been struck silent. This is where I *leave*.

"Well?" I look between the two of them, not moving. "What does 'unmoored' mean?"

"Ghosts don't age unless they choose it," says Brenda. I already know this, but something about her tone tells me to listen. Her words are careful; she's choosing them like she's trying to pick the best shells off a cluttered beach. Delia's mouth stops moving. I wait.

Brenda continues, still slow: "Most people think this means ghosts aren't connected to time anymore. That time doesn't care about the dead, and maybe that's true, in a sense, but it's also false, in a much larger one. Time *needs* the dead, or it gets . . . confused. That's the best way to say it. Time gets confused. Time doesn't run right without the dead to tell it which way it's supposed to go. Ghosts are the nails in the coffin of eternity, and they keep the lid from flying off."

"If there were no ghosts in Manhattan, maybe Tuesday would come after Wednesday instead of before," says Delia, finding her voice. "Or maybe Tuesday would come and never end, and nobody would notice, because who really pays attention to such things? Everything would get tangled, and even the people who couldn't tell you why it hurt to be here would feel the pain of it all. They'd start leaving. That's the long and the short of it. When a place comes altogether unmoored, life deserts it."

"How did people ever go anywhere new? That doesn't make sense. Who was mooring Manhattan before humans got here?"

"Remember the rats," says Brenda. "Everything that lives can die, and everything that dies can leave a ghost behind."

Her meaning catches like fire, immolating me as I stand, wide-eyed from the possibilities. Ghosts of stately old trees lining the coast. Ghosts of whales sounding in the deep water. Even ghosts of mosquitoes, landing on human skin, sipping minutes along with blood, disappearing into eternity before they could be slapped away. And before them, the ghosts of bacteria, of protozoa, of the single-celled swimmers in the primordial sea. The world was a haunted house long before people came along to rattle their chains and wear their winding shrouds.

I ask the only question I can think of, under the circumstances: "Are there dinosaur ghosts?"

Brenda laughs. I slant a glance at her, sure that she's not making fun of me, and she smiles. "I asked the same question, after the corn started talking to me," she says. "My gran was a cotton witch. She didn't know the ways of silk and stalk, but she knew what it was when the fields called you home, and she'd been waiting for a while for me to find my calling. She said there were dinosaur ghosts, once, before people got all scientific about it. Started trying to put names and labels on them, instead of just respecting them as the restless dead. So all the dinos pulled in their remaining years a few centuries ago, and left this world for the next one. Pity. I'd have loved to have seen one."

"Wow," I say.

"But we're off the point," says Brenda, smile fading. "As near as I can tell, you and Delia are the last human ghosts on the island of Manhattan, and that means she needs to stay here, lock the door, and keep herself safe until the city can make itself a few more nails."

That isn't as heartless as it sounds. People die in New York every day. Not just people, either. Pigeons and cats and Sophie's beloved rats. Knowing what I know now, even the cockroaches count. Manhattan would have more nails in short order and be better anchored for having them.

But old ghosts are stronger than new ghosts. They have more practice at moving time from one place to another, channeling the needs of the world through themselves. Delia will still need to stay here. A thousand cockroach ghosts wouldn't equal one of her. I can tell myself that they would be enough, but I'd just be lying to myself and delaying the inevitable. Delia has to stay.

I've always been the one who runs. Maybe it's time I started running for home.

"It's a long way to Mill Hollow," I say.

Brenda nods understanding. "I'll drive."

9

Home Again

Brenda drives a pickup truck the color of bleached corn husks, where it isn't the color of the virulent rust that's eaten through half the frame. She drives like the highway is another rutted dirt road in the middle of Indiana: no haste, no hurry, and yet somehow, no problems. The traffic melts away at our approach, leaving us with a clear bead on the horizon. The speed is enough of a surprise that I don't object when she takes as many surface streets and back roads as the route allows, driving past family farms and through fields of things I can't identify.

"It's been a hard season," she says, eyes on the road, trees rustling around us. We're back on the main road for a while, making the transition between states. "Not enough rain, not enough water, not enough love to fold back into the soil. Some of these folks are on the verge of losing their farms. Some of them have already lost; they're just hanging on and hoping the banks don't notice for a couple years more. Everything's a haunted house in today's America. Everything's in need of an exorcism."

"The world's changed," I say, uncomfortable, not sure what she's trying to tell me.

Brenda sighs. "I know. I guess I don't always make sense to you, and I'm sorry for that. You're a lot younger than I am."

"Always will be, I guess, unless my dying day says I was supposed to be a great-grandmother when I went."

"Age isn't the same as getting older," says Brenda. "You can be here for a thousand years, and you'll still never be as old as I am. Be grateful for that. There's a lot of mourning to be had when you've been alive as long as someone like me. I remember when this land was all about the farms, and the fields went on this side of forever. These days, everyone wants to eat, but no one wants to take the time and care needed to coax the land into giving up its glories. People don't change. We're always selfish, and we're always hungry. We've just gotten better at looking at greed and saying 'Oh, that's self-interest, that's all right.' We've forgotten the way the word 'enough' feels on the tongue."

"Oh." There isn't a place for me in this conversation: Brenda may leave pauses, but they're just breaks in a wall she built years ago, maybe before I was even born. I don't have the strength or the knowledge to get through to her, and so I do the only thing I can, and change the topic. "Have you ever been to Kentucky before?"

"Not in decades."

"Same here." But I can taste it on the back of my tongue, humidity like fine wine, the unique blend of coal and ash and soft green moss that saw me through my childhood, anchored and cushioned me through the blows of my living days. Kentucky is the sound of dogs baying outside the window, the buzz of crickets, and the sweet comfort of Patty's lips against my forehead, kissing my nightmares away. Kentucky is water and soil and doing for ourselves, even when people say things are easier in the cities, that we could have leisure and peace and silence if we were willing to slice ourselves off at the roots and turn into American tumbleweeds, rolling across the plains, looking for a place to grow. Maybe those people are right. Maybe if we'd moved, Patty would have lived, and if Patty had lived, I would have lived too. We could have grown old together instead of rotting away in matching graves.

But those people, those people who lived . . . they wouldn't have been us. We needed Kentucky. It was in our blood and in our bones. Patty had sadness in her bones too, and she needed more than we knew how to give. When the world got to be too much, she left, and I don't see how a change of scene could have saved her.

New York didn't save her. We needed Mill Hollow like Mill Hollow needed us, and every member of my family is buried there, going back to the land that loved us.

"You know things will have changed since you left," says Brenda. Her voice is soft, but when I glance her way, her eyes are fixed on the horizon, as cold and inhuman as the rippling corn that calls her. "It's still your home, but it won't be the same."

"That's all right," I say. "I'm not the same either." When I left I was Jenna who runs, Jenna who buried her sister in the dark Kentucky soil, Jenna who knew hunger and weariness and fear, but who had never known how bad those things could get, even as she saw the sadness growing in her sister's heart. That sadness swallowed Patty like a snake swallows a mouse, and that Jenna fled Kentucky on incorporeal feet, looking for a place where she'd be safe. She never quite managed to find it, and I buried her in the streets of New York, where I learned to be someone new. Someone stronger. Someone who doesn't need to run.

Brenda nods, and we drive in silence for a while, the fields stretching out around us, and the black smudges of the mountains drawing themselves in charcoal and dream across the sky.

Eventually, I sleep. Even dead, that's something I can't help. And maybe it's how close we're coming to

Kentucky—how close I am to home—but for the first time in years, my dreams are clear as crystal and so close that it feels like I can touch them. I dream about my apartment, about my cats, warm and soft and slipping away in comfort. I dream about Delia and Sophie sitting at Delia's kitchen table, the shy rat witch holding a mug of tea, jewel-bright eyes twinkling through the tangles of her hair. Most of all, I dream of Patty walking just ahead of me, hands outstretched, beckoning me home.

When I wake, the car is parked on the soft shoulder of the road, and everything through the windshield is green, green spreading out as far as the eye can see. The sky is dark, but the green shows through. That shouldn't be possible—and as I form the thought, I realize I'm still insubstantial from sleep, still wrapped in my winding shroud. The green is bleeding into the black-and-white world where the dead exist when we don't walk among the living.

Opening the car door would require me to become solid. Passing through it requires nothing at all, and so I drift out into the night, where the air smells of loam and growing things, and the wind whistles softly across that star-studded sky.

Drifting through the corn is odd. It feels like it grabs and snatches at my substance, adding resistance where there should be none. I press onward, listening for signs that I'm not alone. I'm dead. I've been dead for decades. I shouldn't be unnerved by this sort of thing anymore. The part of me in charge of making such decisions is willing to acknowledge the logic of that thought, but it's not willing to stop drawing the skin on my arms into goosebumps, or stop making the hair on the back of my neck stand on end. I don't have a body anymore. Having physiological responses seems unfair.

Then I drift between the rows, and there's Brenda, a black-and-white sketch of a woman sitting cross-legged in the green, her guitar in her lap, her fingers making silent chords. She looks up and smiles.

"Good," she says. "I was wondering when you were going to wake up."

I drift forward, until the last of the cornstalks leaves my body, and let my feet drop to the earth, weighted down by my sudden solidity. The sky takes on the faintest edge of midnight purple; Brenda becomes more difficult to see, washed out by the starlight, still virtually monochrome. The corn is the biggest surprise. The green vanishes, becoming gray in the moonlight, suddenly awash in shadows. The smell of it remains all around us.

"Where are we?"

"About ten miles from Mill Hollow. I wanted you to be awake when we crossed the county line. I've never driven a ghost all the way home before, and there's no telling what sort of thing could happen when we get there."

"Really?"

Brenda shrugs, fingers still moving on her guitar. "Stranger things have happened." The corn rustles. Stranger things are happening right now.

I glance around. "Whose field is this?"

"All cornfields belong to themselves. Farmers are just their temporary caretakers, until the time comes for the harvest to turn everything around." Brenda looks down at her guitar, at her fingers, like she's never seen them before. "I haven't been in a proper field since Bill died. I hadn't realized how much of myself I'd left behind, in silk and stalk and kernel."

"You're sort of freaking me out here."

Brenda's laugh is a bell ringing in a church at midnight. "Aren't you the dead one, while I'm the widow in the weeds? You're supposed to be the monster in the back of the closet, not me."

"When I was a little girl, we knew all about witches, and that you couldn't keep them out of your house if they wanted to come in and steal you away," I say. "We didn't believe in them so much, but it was always fun to pretend. Fear's nice, when it's on purpose. Ghosts, though. We knew ghosts couldn't hurt us if we covered the mirrors when somebody'd gone, and went to visit our dead in the graveyard proper every Easter Sunday."

"Were you a church family?"

"Not exactly." There was always so much to be done, with the four of us on our little farm, and me being the sort of kid who never found a mud puddle she didn't want to be neck-deep in. If there'd been sons, maybe. It was more seemly to work boys to the bone. Patty and I did our share of chores, but we still had time to play and gossip and sit with our parents, Patty reading, me conducting elaborate imaginary scenarios with my dolls. "We made it on the big days, like Christmas, but for the most part, there wasn't time for that sort of thing."

"I see." Brenda keeps looking at her guitar. "Bill and I, we were churchgoers, even with both of us being corn witches. A Jack and a Jenny and our pastor was never any the wiser. I don't think Father Paul would have minded, really. He was as tied to the land as any of us, just in a different way. We raised three children in that parish. Buried one. And then I buried Bill, and my children were grown, and it was time to leave the corn behind."

"Why are you . . ."

"I'm tired, kiddo. I'm older than you, remember? I'm tired, and I haven't gone into the corn for a long time, and I thought this would make me stronger, but all it's done is make me realize how much I want to *rest*." She finally looks at me. Her eyes are bleak. "I'm tired."

There's earning and there's *earned*; there's working for a thing because you feel like you have to pay your dues, and then there's realizing the work itself pays the bill. I offer her my hands before I can think better of it, and when she lets go of her guitar and takes them, I pull her to her feet, my skin touching hers.

Her eyes widen as she realizes what I've done, but it's too late. I can feel the year I've taken settling over me, thickening my bones, freckling my skin, extending my hair a few inches past my shoulders. I'm not twenty-six and change anymore. I'm twenty-seven, on the downward stretch toward thirty, and when Brenda drops my hands and starts to scold me, I don't really hear her, because I can see it, *I can see it*, my dying day, shimmering in the distance like a promise, like a prayer, like my mother's hands easing me into bed at the end of a long day.

"Four years, eleven months, three weeks, four days," I say, and my voice is thick with wonder and dismay, until there's no picking the two apart.

Brenda stops, staring at me. Finally, she asks, "Are you seeing your due date?"

"My dying day. Yes. Yes, I can see it. I can *see* it." I turn back to her, beaming bright. "I'm almost there. I keep working hard, I'll be there before I know it."

"You going to keep that year you took?" Brenda holds up her hand, studying it like she could see a difference.

At my age, a year changes everything. At her age, a year is just one more page in the back half of a novel, blending seamlessly into the whole.

"Unless you want it back."

"I thought you had to earn everything you took."

"I talked to two witches and hosted a house party, and I'm going back to the Hollow," I say. "That's earning enough for me. Besides, I'm going to need you at your best, and I know having time taken helps."

"Sometimes I wish witches left ghosts, just so there'd be some of you who understood how damn *tempting* you are," says Brenda. She balls her hands into fists for a moment before she stands. It was only a year, but she's moving more easily than she did before, smooth and confident, like she knows the ground will be there when she moves her feet. With a year gone and the preternatural thrill of its removal thrumming in her veins, she looks like queen of the corn. She looks like she could take on the world.

I look at her, and I don't shy away. I am not Jenna-who-runs anymore. I can't afford to be. That means I can't be Jenna-who-refuses, either. Taking the year strengthened both of us. I have to keep it. "I have a bit of an understanding," I say. "You done here?"

"No," says Brenda. "But I'm close enough that I can come with you. I'll be back soon enough, I think. My bones have had enough of steel and concrete. It's time I went out into the green."

"Then we're both going home," I say, and turn and walk away. A second passes before Brenda follows, and we move together through the corn, the ghost and the witch, and I can hear Mill Hollow calling me, and oh, Patty, Patty, I am almost there.

After all these years and all these miles, I am finally coming home.

10

Do What I Tell You To

It takes surprisingly little time to cover the last ten miles between me and Mill Hollow. It feels like it should take eternity, like this is the sort of grand quest that must be undertaken only with the greatest solemnity and care, not by a witch in an ancient pickup and a dead girl who feels like she's going to be sick.

Then we come around a curve in the road and there it is, beckoning me home:

MILL HOLLOW, KY

POPULATION 220 · ELEVATION 1,170 FEET

WE'RE HAPPY THAT YOU'RE HERE

Brenda pulls off on the shoulder of the highway, killing the engine and twisting in her seat to look at me expectantly. "Well?" she asks. "Get out of the car."

The hesitation is writ in every line of my body, in the stillness of my hands and my reluctance to meet her eyes. "Do I have to?"

"Yes. We don't know what's going to happen when you cross the line, and I'd rather it didn't happen in my car."

I sigh, but there's nothing yielding in her: she looks at me calmly, and waits, until I reach for the door handle and let myself out, into the pitch-black night. Then I stop, steadying myself against the body of the truck. The cornfield was overwhelming: it was green and growth and *hers*, even if those stalks had grown in good Kentucky soil. But this . . .

This is Mill Hollow. This is the sound of insects in the trees, the hoot of owls, the distant whisper of the creek as it runs between the roots of trees so much older than I am that they probably never noticed I was here, much less mourned when I was gone. This is home. This is where I lived; this is where I died. This is everything I ever had, and everything I gave away.

The skin of my palm is tingling, and it's somehow no surprise when I glance over and see that it has slipped below the surface of the truck. I'm insubstantial in this moment, a memory pretending to be a girl. I can't breathe. It's a good thing that I don't need to. All I can do is stand, frozen, and let the night roll over me, washing me away.

I am finally, finally, home.

I step away from the truck and walk under my own power over the borderline, into Mill Hollow. I stop there, waiting for Brenda to start the truck up again and come to meet me. Nothing catches fire. Brenda finally drives those few precious feet, looking out the window, and asks, "You okay, Jenna?"

"It's still here," I say. "I never really believed ... I went away. I always thought it went away too."

"The past has a way of hanging on, even when we think it's dead and buried," says Brenda. "Looks like you're not going to explode. Get back in the truck. We need to find Danny. Any chance you can track him from here?"

"No," I say, climbing back into my seat. "I knew he was here because this is the Hollow; this is mine. But that doesn't mean I have a map of the place tattooed on the inside of my eyelids."

"It was worth a try," she says philosophically. The truck rumbles around us, and we roll onward, into Mill Hollow.

Manhattan may not be the biggest city in the world, but it feels like it is: the city that never sleeps, the "Big Apple," all those fancy names people slap on it as they struggle to put the feeling of vastness, of restlessness, of *potential* into something they can hold onto. It's possible to stand at the corner of Fourteenth and Broadway and believe that when humanity is over, this city, or the ghost of this city, will be all that remains.

Mill Hollow ... Mill Hollow is the other side of that coin. It's silence. It's stillness. It's the feeling of eyes watching from the empty trees, knowing that frogs and owls and creeping night-things have their full attention fixed on you. If Manhattan is the light, Mill Hollow is the shadow, and it's never been possible for one to exist without the other. Kentucky is a long way from New York, but distance, like time, is as much a convenience as anything else. This is my home. This has always been my home. The only reason I was able to stay away so long is that I was living in the other half of it, living in the light, but I never forgot the shadow. I never could.

Brenda keeps her eyes mostly on the road as she drives, following the black, winding path through the trees. There are no streetlights here, and the branches are tight-knit above us, blocking out starlight and moonlight alike. "You okay?"

"I'm fine." I'm lying. I don't have the words to tell the truth. How do you put something like this into words? You don't, that's how. But every breath I take pulls Mill Hollow deeper into my lungs, and even if my body no longer strips the oxygen from the air, it still appreciates the reminder. I feel like I can do anything. I feel like I can fly.

"Any thoughts on where Danny would be? I've never been here before."

"I haven't been here in twenty years."

Brenda's laugh is swift and mocking. "What, you're expecting me to believe this is a place that changes quickly? I'm from a small town. I know how they work. Whatever you're thinking was here twenty years ago will probably still be here today."

"Not everything." Patty is gone. My parents are gone. The things that matter most about the Hollow are underground and resting peacefully . . . but in a way, that means Brenda's right, because they're still here. They're never going to leave. I'm still here too. I never left, not in body, not in bone. Dusk or dark or dawn or day, I've been here the whole time.

Silence falls between us, too heavy with things unsaid to be companionable, stretched too thinly to be comfortable. I look out the window on the blackness, and say, slowly, "Danny never liked to go where ghosts would be. He said being dead was a clerical error, and he didn't approve one bit. So he wouldn't be in the graveyard. There might be a comic book store in town. There wasn't one twenty years ago."

"I doubt it," says Brenda. "Town with less than three hundred people, you can't keep the doors open on a specialty store like that. He'll be somewhere else."

"I know." I want to say he's at my family home; I want to give myself an excuse to go there, to peer through the windows and search for some sign of what my family has become. I can't. Danny wouldn't go there.

Why would Danny come *here*? He's from California; he crossed the country to hide from the circumstances of his death. He ran *away* from who he'd been when he was alive, and most people don't run to places like Mill Hollow. Even some of our neighbors don't know we exist. We're a footnote in the history of the state, one more tiny tick of a town clinging to the ridge of the mountains for as long as we can before the Appalachians shake us off, roll over, and go back into their dog-dreaming slumber. I've never mentioned the Hollow to Danny, not when we spoke in public, not when we spoke in private, not *ever*. Delia knows where I'm from, but she wouldn't have told him. She wouldn't have had a reason to. Ghosts don't tell tales out of school where other ghosts are concerned. There are too few of us for that, and the dead hold grudges.

"He's not alone." The words make so much sense, spoken aloud, that it's difficult to understand how I didn't see it before now. But then, this isn't the sort of thing I do; this isn't the sort of story I belong in. I glance toward Brenda. She's nodding. "Someone had to bring him here," I say, and hate the words. "But why Mill Hollow? Why my hometown?"

"You're an old ghost, as human ghosts go." My surprise must show, because Brenda takes her eyes off the road long enough to offer me an apologetic grimace. "Sorry, kiddo, but it's true. Most people are greedy when it comes to moving on. They grab all the time they need, give their weeping relatives a little youth as a going-away present, and head into whatever comes next. You'll always have ghosts like Delia—she's going to outlast us all—and the few who stick around for centuries, but most ghosts? Nah. They realize what they are, they haunt the living for a few years, and then they're done. They want to know what comes next. Hanging out here is like spending all your time in the parking lot at Disney World, and then deciding never to go inside."

"I've never been to Disney World," I say. I can't think of anything else.

Brenda laughs. "Too late now, I'm afraid. So many dead people were making their pilgrimages to the Happiest Place on Earth that it was throwing the numbers off. Disney started taking fingerprints, and when that didn't work, they went to this new system where they tag all their guests like migrating cattle. No little electronic gadget on your wrist, no amusement park for you. Not too late for Disneyland, though, if you wanted to head for California. Just do it soon. Disney's done letting ghosts ride for free."

I'm not sure which is more disturbing: the idea that ghosts would flock to Disney World in such numbers that it would become a problem, or the thought of Disney knowing enough about the dead to do something about it. I shake my head, trying to clear the thought away. "What does me being an old ghost have to do with anything?"

"Delia stayed in Manhattan so that it wouldn't become unmoored. She wouldn't have needed to do that if her family hadn't buried her out in Babylon—a town in Connecticut. Far enough away from New York that she can't go back to her grave without losing her grasp on her chosen home. You're too young to be an anchor for a place the size of Manhattan. But Mill Hollow? You can anchor Mill Hollow just fine."

"How can I anchor Mill Hollow? I haven't been here in forty years."

"You've never left, remember? Your bones have been here this whole time. Your bones could have been keeping the town anchored to the world while your spirit's been haunting other halls. If there were no other human ghosts here, you would have been the nail around which everything revolves. A small-town ghost, known to be haunting a big city? Oh, darling. You painted the target on your own map."

I stare at her. "You're not making any sense."

Brenda's headlights illuminate a stop sign, red and white and gray with dust from the mines. She could probably blow right through it at this hour of the night, but she stops anyway, twisting in her seat to face me. Her expression is grave.

"There are two ways a ghost can anchor a place to the world. The active way, that's what Delia is doing in Manhattan. At the same time, as long as she's a haunt and in the world of the living, she's also a passive anchor for Babylon, where she's buried. That's why witches and ghosts don't fight more than we do. If we needed you to stay where you were buried, there'd be a lot more 'Sorry, but I have to bind you into this oak tree for the sake of everyone I love.' Nimue did Merlin, just like the legends say. What they miss is that Merlin was dead at the time, and if he'd gone chasing dishware across Europe, he'd have been leaving Camelot without an anchor. His bones were long gone, you see, and he allowed no other ghosts to haunt his hallowed halls. So you've been haunting New York, and all this time your bones have been here, comfortable in the soil, part of what's anchoring Mill Hollow."

"Why does that explain Danny being here?"

"Because a town this small is highly unlikely to have more than one human ghost. As long as you were in Manhattan, Mill Hollow was the safest place for him to go. Already anchored, but with no one to ask why he was in town. Him, and whoever he's working for."

"You mean the witch." That is the long and the short

of it. Danny is a ghost, and ghosts can't do much to their own kind. We can't prison ourselves in glass, can't trade time between us. For those things, you need a witch. And the ghosts of Manhattan are missing.

"I do." Brenda looks at me seriously. "This is your town, Jenna. This is your holy ground."

"No," I say, without thinking. "It's not. I'm not the anchor here." Because I can sort of see what she's trying to say—the shape of it, at least—and what she's saying is wrong. Maybe I'm the oldest human ghost in Mill Hollow, but that doesn't make me the anchor. There's something else holding this place to the world. Something other than me.

"Maybe so and maybe not, but it's still your town. If there was a witch here, where would she be hiding? Where would we find her?"

There will be time to argue about anchors later. I close my eyes, breathing in the taste of Kentucky, the sweet dampness that coats my lungs and stays behind even when the air rushes out again, unchanged by its time in the phantom prison of my lungs.

As I breathe, I start to see the Hollow sketched across the inside of my eyes, a pale, monochrome map of a place. There's the graveyard, where my bones lie next to Patty's, whiling away eternity in a pine box. There's the church, where we went on special Sundays, promising to honor and obey a God we didn't quite understand and didn't quite believe in. There's home, and the school, and the narrow strip of shops that was our main street, and the old theater, and—

Stop. Back up. The theater I remember was the jewel of the town, small and bright and always open, with cheap matinees for the kids and long engagements of the hits for the adults. Patty and I went there about once a week when we were growing up, trading our pocket money for the chance at escape, even if it was only for a little while. I'm pretty sure that's where she fell in love with the idea of New York, turning it into the fairy-tale ending that could save her from the monsters in her mind. That's where I fell in love with the idea of running. Running so far, so fast, that the sunset could never catch me and the movie would never have to end.

But the theater on the inside of my eyelids is shabby and shuttered, with boards across the windows and nothing written on the marquee. I know the reasons why even without thinking about them. Cheap cable, home video, a dwindling population, and better places for the money to go as the ticket prices soared. It makes *sense* that the Mill Hollow Cinema would be closed down. I still never expected to see it, not in my lifetime, and not in what came after.

"The theater," I say, opening my eyes. "That's where

they'll be." I can't put words to why I'm so sure. I just *know*. The Mill Hollow Cinema is dark, and shuttered, and filled with shadows. It's also right at the center of town, with multiple rooms far from the street. Someone who could get inside there could hide for weeks, if they stayed out of the lobby and away from the windows.

"You're sure?"

I shake my head. "I'm not sure of anything anymore. But it feels . . . it feels right. I guess that matters, under the circumstances."

"I guess it does," Brenda agrees. "Which way?"

I tell her, the directions coming as quick and easy as a breeze that's been waiting years to blow. As I speak, I crank down my window, letting the smell of Mill Hollow fill the cab from top to bottom. Brenda looks at me thoughtfully for a moment before mimicking the gesture, until the wind blows clear through, carrying everything the Hollow has to offer us. I can even smell corn. Small patches, not sprawling, endless acres, but that seems to be enough to put some soldier in her spine; she's sitting straighter when she hauls on the wheel and sends us rolling toward town, her eyes fixed on the windshield and the distant fight to come.

"Danny usually did a good job of hiding that he was dead," I say. "How did he get mixed up in this?"

"He's working with a witch," says Brenda. "Thing

about witches is we can always spot the dead when we find them up and walking around. It's how I found you. Whoever it is wouldn't have to have been looking for a corporeal haunt. They could have just been walking past the comic book store and spotted him out of the corner of their eye, and the rest is horrible history."

"How come you can see us and we can't see you?" The question has frustrated me for years. I don't make any effort to hide that as I fire it at Brenda, eyes narrowed and lip pushed outward in the beginning of a pout. "It's not fair."

"You say that like somebody put this system together on purpose," says Brenda. There's no rancor in her tone. "We don't have checks and balances, Jenna. We don't have a system of countermeasures to avoid abuse of power. Witches can see ghosts, ghosts can't see witches. Witches can't see each other, either. We're shadows on the wall of the world, and we find each other *through* abuses of power, half the time. Trees start dying, or lambs are born with two heads . . ."

"Or all the ghosts go missing," I say softly.

"That, too," Brenda agrees. "It's not fair, all right? If it were, you wouldn't have witches like Sophie, who can barely keep herself together on the good days. You wouldn't have corn witches born in cities and steel witches born in small towns with nothing taller than the church spire. It happens because it happens. The universe isn't fair."

"Ugh." I drop my head into my hands. I can't see much of anything, anyway; it's too dark out there, and maybe that's a mercy. The Hollow still smells like home, but I'm smart enough to know that time changes a place. It won't look like home when the sun comes up. It'll look like someplace else, someplace almost familiar, someplace impossibly strange.

I should never have come here. That's the long and the short of it. I should have stayed in New York with Delia, walled up in my apartment, taking care of my cats, and not putting myself into the line of fire. I'm Jenna-who-runs. I don't belong here.

But I'm not Jenna-who-runs anymore. I've put her aside, and some of the ghosts who've gone missing are my friends. I would want them to look for me, even if it meant going back to their personal versions of Mill Hollow, the towns and cities they've left behind as they roved out from their graves. I would want them to *care*. That means I have to. And besides . . .

"We don't know that Danny is here voluntarily," I say, raising my head. "Any ghost who's been around more than a few years knows not to fight with witches if you don't want to wind up prisoned in glass. This witch could be forcing him to do this."

"Yes, they could," says Brenda. "They might not be, though. Danny could be doing this of his own free will."

The thought is chilling. "I don't know why he would."

"Why does anyone do anything?" asks Brenda. "That's one thing the living, the dead, and the witching have in common: the mind is a mystery to all of us. Maybe he resents the fact that he died. Maybe the witch made him promises they don't intend to keep. Maybe it's something else altogether. I knew one witch from Arizona who worked with his own great-grandmother to defraud people. Held séances that always bore fruit, because she was happy to appear when he called her name. People are strange."

"You can say that again," I say. The air carries a faint, sweet scent, like cinnamon. It shouldn't be here, just like we shouldn't be here. I stiffen. "We're almost there."

The town's main street—which seemed so important once upon a time, and now seems little better than an afterthought—is lit up like daylight compared to everything around it. There are streetlights here, six of them, two in front of the gas station and the other four scattered the length of the two-block stretch that constitutes the shopping district. There are a few cars. Most of the shop owners live above their livelihoods. The vet's still here, and so is the doctor, although the names on the signs have changed; it's good to see that the Hollow is still doing well enough to keep those simple luxuries. I hate to think about the people who might have been my neighbors having to drive hours just to have their dogs vaccinated or their appendixes prodded.

The theater is dark, nestled in the stretch between two streetlights, so the shadows can take everything but the box-and-angle shape of it. It squats like a spider, like a predator considering the rest of the street, and I shudder. It seems like it must have always been like this, like the theater can't have changed this much while I was gone, and yet it doesn't fit my memories of the place. I was happy here. I know that much. I was happy.

"Are you ready?" asks Brenda.

We have no plan. We have no preparation. She's a corn witch with no field and I'm a ghost in a place where every piece of glass might be resonant enough to hold me, and we have no chance if Danny has joined forces with someone stronger than we are.

"I guess I have to be," I say.

Brenda pulls up to the sidewalk and stops the truck. She retrieves her guitar from the back as she walks toward the theater, and I follow, a ghost in blue jeans and sneakers, into whatever happens next.

11

Popcorn Dreams on a Silver Screen

The theater door is locked. I glance to Brenda, who nods. I take a breath, and let go. The color rushes out of the world like the tide rushing back out to sea, and I don't need to look at myself to know that I'm insubstantial, half-there, like the memory I've been since the day I died.

Passing through the door is like moving through cobwebs. It has more resistance but less pull than the corn: while it may resent my intrusion, it does not strive to keep me here. In short order I am inside the lobby, surrounded by the shadows of the monochrome reality I've cast myself into. It's dark here. I can still see: ghost eyes are well suited to the dark. Let Brenda wait a moment more. She'll understand once I open the door.

Old posters cling to the lobby walls, pinned like butterflies behind dusty glass. Their preservative prisons haven't protected them completely. They're tattered and peeling at the edges, and none of them is more recent than the late nineties. That's when this place closed its doors. I can't smell anything, but I'm sure the air is thick with decay, and I know that some of the dark patches on the walls are mold, eating through the wallpaper, which must have been infused with butter after so many years sharing the lobby with the popcorn machine. The stairs to the projectionist's booth are still roped off, and I see no clean spots on the fake brass hooks to indicate that anyone has moved the rope in decades. Danny and his witch are on this floor.

There's nothing more to see here, and I don't want to risk wisping around the theater; if the witch spotted me without Brenda to intervene, it would be a quick one-two-three from there to the inside of a mirror. My feet hit the ground as I solidify, and the room goes dark, giving me a moment of absolute terror as I wait for the noise to trigger some attack from one of the silent doors around me.

Nothing comes. I force myself to relax, step forward, and unlock the theater door, opening it so Brenda can slip inside. She brings light with her, pale gold, like corn silk. It doesn't emanate from her body or anything like that; it doesn't seem to have a source at all. It's just *there*, buttery and warm as morning sunlight, slowly growing to illuminate everything around us.

Now that there's color in the world, I can see that the patches on the walls are definitely mold, and that mushrooms are growing through the floor in the corners, making this cavern of cinematic wonders more like something from a horror show. Brenda looks around, and her eyes are sad.

"Must've been nice when it was new" is all she says. She doesn't keep her voice down. I shoot her a startled look, and she smiles, holding up a hand to indicate the cloud of light around us. I can see specks of dust dancing in it, like chaff coming off the fields. "Light costs. I'm trading sound. You can hear me, but no one outside the glow can."

"That sounds less like a payment and more like another advantage."

"The laws of magic, like the laws of nature, are not always as balanced as they might seem."

I don't say anything. I just stare. I've been dead for forty years. I've met dozens of witches, even if I've chosen to hide from most of them rather than risking them grabbing me and stuffing me into a mirror. This—this glow, this cornfield shine that fills the room—is the most real *magic* I've ever seen. Even Sophie's rats can't compare.

Brenda looks around again. "This is your place, not mine," she says. "Where would they be?"

"They're not in the projection booth; no one's touched that rope in years," I say. Even if Danny could pass through it, his witch couldn't. I don't think. Maybe some witches can fly, or turn into smoke, or burst into flocks of birds. All those things feel impossible, things out of fairy tales, but the room is bright when it should be dark. Magic is real. Once magic is real, nothing is entirely out of the question.

"If he was working with a weather witch or any sort of bird witch that involved flight, they'd have gone for the highest available point," says Brenda, and I realize she's been running down a list this whole time, checking off the things that don't fit our situation. You don't find subway witches at street level, and you don't find sky witches on the ground. Everything we find eliminates another hundred possibilities. Maybe that won't be enough to get us to the truth before it's right in front of us, but it's enough to make the choices narrower, and that can equip us both better for what's to come. "Where do the doors go?"

"Um. There are two auditoriums, assuming there was never any renovation." I point to the appropriate doors. "That's the manager's office, and that's the supply closet. They keep, you know, the popcorn and butter and stuff in there." Or they did, back when this was a theater and not a crypt. If I drifted through that door now, I'd find a mono-chrome horror of either rotting food or empty shelves. Nothing I'd want to see or remember. It's a relief knowing they probably won't be in there. The space is too small to be comfortable, and while Danny might be fine with a standing coffin of a hideaway, I doubt his witch would be.

Brenda's thoughts follow the same trail as mine. She dismisses the pantry and focuses on the other three doors. "Are there bathrooms?"

"Back of the theater. Not big. They always smelled sort of like swamp water, even in the middle of the summer, when you'd figure that they'd dry out all the way."

"So that's not a good hideout. Is there a back door?"

"There's the service door on the other side of the pantry. It feeds into the alley next to the building. That's probably how they've been getting in and out without attracting attention from the rest of the town." Danny can float through walls, but I've never heard of a witch with that particular power, and if that were a risk, Brenda would have said something by now. I hope.

"All right," says Brenda. "Let's go."

The first auditorium is empty of everything but ripped red velvet seats, now stained with patchwork swirls of mold, and the blind eye of the old movie screen, which stares in eternal, silent judgement over the room. A rat squeaks, startled by our presence, and runs by at the back of the stage that supports the screen. I wrinkle my nose.

"Ew."

"They're not here," says Brenda, and we move on.

The second auditorium is in worse shape than the first. Someone—vandals, or a hopeful salvage company—ripped half the chairs from the floor before abandoning them in the corner where they remain, filthy and strewn with cobwebs. Naked, rotting hardwood slats sit where the chairs used to be bolted to the floor. I can see through into the tarry blackness of the basement below, and I am all too aware of the weight of our steps on the rotten wood. Sure, I'm already dead, but that doesn't mean I'd enjoy the fall. I'd need to turn insubstantial halfway down or risk making a racket that could bring this whole house of cards tumbling down.

There's a sleeping bag on the corner of the stage, incongruous in its modern nylon brightness. A camp lantern sits next to it, bulb dim. Brenda lifts the handle with one finger. When she lets it go, it clinks back down against the lid with a dull, tinny sound, like a fork being hit against the side of a can of peaches.

"Someone here's alive," she says. "There's no food. Either they're out scavenging, or this is just a way station and they're not staying here full-time."

It feels like there should be a third option, like I'm missing something. I inhale, and the room carries the faint, distant smell of swamp, just like the bathrooms always have. There's something beneath the dank slime-scent of rot and mud and loam, something that belongs here and shouldn't be here at the same time. I breathe in again, and frown. It smells green. It smells like Brenda, and the corn.

"The mirrors aren't here," I say. Something is wrong. I don't want to be here. "I'm going to check the manager's office."

"Be careful," says Brenda.

"I will." I need to be: there's a witch somewhere near here who enjoys prisoning ghosts in glass, and I'm in Mill Hollow. Every mirror in this town is a danger to me. I also don't need to be careful, because all the mirrors in this theater are already being used. Can't cram more than one ghost into the same glass without cracking it. That's why mirrors can be uncovered after a little time has passed between the funeral and the taking down. If a ghost was going to wander by, they're already in there.

It's dark in the lobby without Brenda, but I know this building like I know my own hand, and I'm dead: I'm not afraid of the dark. I walk, quick and sure, to the manager's office, and pause before reaching for the doorknob, taking a moment to close my eyes and sniff the air. It still smells of the green. Brenda isn't in this room, and yet it still smells of the green, of the cornfield, roots in the earth and ears in the sky. Something isn't right.

The door isn't locked. I twist the knob until it clicks, the latch letting go and allowing me to step through. It's no surprise, somehow, to find that the back wall is gone, leaving a gaping hole that looks out on the vast stretch of tangled grass and incipient swampland behind the theater. There were big development plans for all this, once. The people who owned the theater were going to sit on the land until Mill Hollow became the booming coal town it was always meant to be, and then they were going to sell big and profitable, retire on the proceeds to someplace fancy and far away, like Ann Arbor.

I always knew that was a lie. Even if they could have sold—even if the price of coal had continued to rise and the mine had suddenly become twice as successful as it had ever been, even when it was bright and new and the environmental groups hadn't started sniffing around—they would never have been able to leave Mill Hollow. Only the young ever really left, and half of them still came creeping back, tails between their legs, unable to put the shadow of the mountain and the memory of ghosts in glass aside.

That's what I always expected Patty to do. That's why I was sad but not afraid when she left me behind. And now here I am, forty years gone, and the field's still here, because the boom never came; the boom is never coming, not here.

There's something wrong with the grass. I take a step outside, and another, and another, until I'm standing in what should be kudzu and brush, and somehow it towers around me, taller than I am, blocking out the sky. Corn. I'm standing in a sea of corn, stalks rustling as far as the eye can see, and everything is green, blocking out even the smell of the Hollow itself. No no *no*. This isn't right. This isn't real. This isn't—

"I thought I told you to stay in Manhattan, Jenna." Danny's voice is soft and apologetic. I turn and there he is, standing behind me with his hands jammed into his pockets and an apologetic look on his face, like he can't believe he has to do this. "You weren't supposed to be here. You were never supposed to be here."

"Danny." There's no surprise in my voice, no relief, only dull acknowledgement. I've known he was in Mill Hollow since he called my apartment. It only makes sense that he would be here now. "What's going on? Where are all the other ghosts?"

"You're about to find out." The voice is unfamiliar, but when I look toward it, the face is one I almost know. Her chin is rounder than Brenda's, her forehead higher and her ears smaller, but she has her mother's eyes, and her mother's tight, thin-lipped mouth. There's a mirror in her hand. I recognize it from Patty's vanity, many years and not so many miles from here.

Then she holds it up, and the glass is big enough to swallow the world, and everything is gone. Even the corn.

12

By the Birchwood Bed

Piece by piece and sliver by sliver, I come back to myself, piecing mind and memory together one shard at a time. It feels like I'm trying to do a jigsaw made entirely of broken glass, all without opening my eyes, but I'm managing it. With every piece that slides into place, a bit more of who I am comes back into the light, until finally, I find the piece that is my eyes, and I open them on a world gone silver.

It's not the monochrome of being insubstantial; it's *gilded,* covered in a layer of gleaming metallic light, like the world has been dipped in glitter. I raise my hand, holding it in front of my face. It isn't there. There isn't even a glow. It's like I've been wiped from reality, even though I'm still here, still thinking, still feeling, still aware of my surroundings. Everything is silent, motionless. With my deletion from the world, even when I move, nothing else does.

With dim horror, I realize what's happened.

I've been prisoned in glass.

As if the realization has triggered something, light floods my cage, bathing everything in brilliant white. I throw up an arm I can't see to shield my eyes. It doesn't do any good. Invisible flesh is not a good thing to hide behind.

A woman's face appears, as huge as one of the stars on the old theater's screen. She's smirking. I hate her. "Hello, little ghost. You know, you're the only one who's tracked me down. Where's the sense in that, huh? You must really hate yourself. Is this how ghosts commit suicide?"

"Go to hell."

She raises an eyebrow. She can hear me, then; the glass goes both ways. That's a relief. I may be toothless in here, but at least she hasn't gagged me. "Feisty, aren't you? I'd peg you at what, mid-twenties right now? That's fine. You're good for at least another seventy years."

"What are you talking about? How did you get my sister's mirror? Let me out of here!"

My porthole shifts as the mirror is moved, and I find myself looking out at a sheepish Danny. "Sorry, Jenna," he says, refusing to meet my eyes. "You could have stayed in New York. I mean, you didn't have to do this."

"Let me out of here. Danny—Danny! Look at me. You know this isn't right. You know that ghosts don't belong in glass. *Danny!* Let me out!" Maybe he can see me, even if I can't see myself. I wave my arms, trying to get his attention, trying to make him look at me.

He doesn't. Instead, he looks to the unnamed witch with Brenda's eyes, and says, "Jenna was the coffin nail for this town. We can't stick around here if you've got her in that mirror."

To my surprise, she laughs. "Oh, no, that's where you're wrong. People think so linearly. She's not the one keeping Mill Hollow moored. There's an old oak's ghost in the deepest part of the hollow, two hundred years old and still haunting. She's extraneous. Humans are not always the most important thing in the world. We're staying, and we're having our market, and that's that." She tilts my mirror back toward her face, frowning as she touches the skin near her eye. "Think I could do with a little less age on me before the auctions begin?"

"You've bled twenty years in the last two weeks," says Danny. "None of your clothes fit right anymore."

"I know, isn't it wonderful?" She laughs. "All right, little ghost. Dazzle me."

I don't want to do this, *I don't want to do this,* and I have no choice: she has me prisoned in glass. Her fingers touch the mirror's surface and I bleed the time off of her, leaving her fresh-faced and gasping with pleasure. I manage to stop myself shy of my dying day, but barely. This woman, this witch, has forced me to take the rest of the time I had coming to me. It shouldn't hurt. It does.

If I get out of the mirror now, I can't move on. Not without giving her time away.

"There," she says, smiling as she takes her hand away from her face. "I'll be able to afford to go shopping very soon. Anything I want can be mine. You have no idea how lucrative this sort of thing can be."

"You're *selling* us?" I can't keep the revulsion out of my voice. I don't even want to try. I still ache all the way down to my insubstantial bones from the force of her violation. "You can't do that! We're people!"

"You *were* people," she says. "Now you're just shadows on the wall. Show me where the Constitution says ghosts have rights. Show me the politicians who swear to support their phantom contingent. You die, we bury you, we put the muslin over the mirrors to keep you from getting caught and frightening Grandma to death, and we move on. But you can't. You're just shadows. Shadows don't get to choose their fate like that. If I'm smart enough to figure out how to catch you, if I'm quick enough to come up and get you to look in my glass, why shouldn't I claim you? Shadows need a light to cast them. I can be that light."

"We may not be alive, but we have lives," I snap. "There are people who will miss me."

"I'm sure there are. You're the one who works at the

suicide hotline, aren't you? You know, I never could figure out whether that was noble or petty of you. Keep people from killing themselves too young, keep the ghost population down, stay special." She shakes her head. "It doesn't matter. Busybodies who think answering a phone can change the world are a dime a dozen. They'll replace you with someone who has a pulse, and everyone will be better off."

The world outside my prison shifts again, dizzyingly fast, until it goes away and is replaced by more of the silvery nothingness. She's put my mirror facedown on some surface. I stay frozen where I am, unsure how to walk when I can't see my feet, staring, furious, into the nothingness.

Glass. She's prisoned me in glass, and she's going . . . going to *sell* me? Going to sell *all* of us. I don't need to ask myself why: the motives are clear without thinking about them too deeply. Ghosts take time. Ghosts can reach into a mortal life and make it longer, just by pulling away the time that has already passed. She said I was good for another seventy years, but that's just an estimate, because a ghost prisoned in glass can't move on to whatever comes next. Until the mirror is broken, we're trapped. Whoever buys me—whoever buys us—will be able to use us to stay young and beautiful in a world that's become increasingly obsessed with youth and beauty.

It shouldn't be a surprise that this is happening. The surprise should be that it's taken this long.

"All right, Jenna, pull yourself together," I say. There is no echo here, but there are surfaces, gilded in silver, beckoning me with the illusion of a world. I can't see myself. Do I exist? Closing my eyes changes nothing, so I tilt the idea of my head back until I'm looking upward, then reach out in front of myself and tell my hands to find each other. It's harder than it should be. I've touched my body in the dark a million times since I was born, and even more often since I've died, but I wasn't *thinking* about it then. It was something that just happened. Now I have to feel around, trying to guess where my hands are in a world that has no points of reference—

—until fingers find fingers and interlace, coming together the way hands are meant to. I look back down. I still can't see myself, but now I know, for sure, that I exist; I'm not just a disembodied voice floating in a silver sea. If I exist, I can find a way out of here. I'm sure of that.

The witch is Brenda's daughter. I'm sure of that, too, just like I'm sure Brenda doesn't know. Brenda could be the greatest actress of her age—and there's no real telling what that age is, not with her being a witch, not with ghosts in the world—and she still wouldn't have been able to fool Sophie's rats like that. Sophie wouldn't lie to me. She didn't tell me she was a witch, but that was because she hadn't needed to, and she likes me. Sophie would have told me if Brenda was a danger. Brenda doesn't know her daughter is doing this. That means Brenda might also be in danger.

I've known her a long time. I wouldn't call us old friends, but it's been long enough that I feel like I owe her some sort of help, if I can just figure out how to get the hell out of here.

Being prisoned in glass is the thing every ghost I know fears more than anything. Even exorcism is a small threat compared to that. An exorcised ghost is scattered for a little while, becoming a whisper on the wind and a chilly place in still air. Depending on how strong they are, they'll come back together in a week, a month, a year. The longest exorcism I've ever heard of lasted eighteen months, and half of that was because the ghost in question was so surprised that his meek little wife had been willing to light the candles and chant the words. I've never been exorcised, but the people I know who have say it's like taking a long, restorative nap. Some older ghosts even do it on purpose, just to break up the monotony.

Glass is different. Glass catches and keeps, until someone decides to let you out or the mirror is broken. Glass takes your choices away. If the witch who has me wanted me to take another year off her, or two, or twenty, I wouldn't have a choice. I don't know what happens to a ghost who ages themselves past their dying day, but I've never met anyone who had passed that age and stayed corporeal.

I have to get out of here.

If I have hands, I have feet. I may be walking blind, but the ground seems smooth, and presumably I'll know if I fall. I start walking. When nothing bad happens, I start running.

Dead people don't get tired. There have been a couple of Olympic records set by ghosts, running right alongside the living. I run, and I run, and I run until time doesn't mean anything anymore, time is something for people who exist outside of mirrors, in a world where there are walls, and borders, and consequences.

There's no warning before the silver world in front of me disappears, replaced by Danny's face. I can see the theater behind him, tattered wallpaper and all. There's no sign of the corn. He glances nervously over his shoulder before looking back to the glass and whispering, "Jenna?"

I stop running. There isn't any point. "Let me out of here."

Relief washes over his face. For just that moment, I can remember that he was my friend before this started happening, before he joined forces with a witch and ran for my hometown. Then the relief fades, replaced by regret, and he says, "I can't do that. Teresa would put *me* in a mirror if I did that."

"And your freedom matters more than mine; is that it?"

He doesn't answer. He doesn't need to. The answer is in the situation, in the fact that he would help a witch harm his own kind rather than risk himself sounding the alarm. That's almost being charitable. It assumes she approached him and not the other way around; that he's just a coward and not a traitor.

"Why?" My question is soft, almost gentle; I want him to think he can make me understand.

"It only takes one ghost to anchor a city," says Danny. "I knew Delia would never leave. I managed to make Teresa understand. Nobody who was haunting Manhattan was actually buried there, so we couldn't count on bones; it had to be her. I had her convinced that you were anchoring Mill Hollow. She would have left you alone. She would never have gone looking for a replacement ghost."

"Does everybody know about anchors but me?" I demand, throwing my hands up. Then I pause. Something about the way he said that . . . "What do you mean, a replacement ghost?"

Danny looks uncomfortable. "Forget it."

"No, I won't. What do you mean?"

"Ghosts don't just *happen*. Someone has to make them. That's why we all died so early, and why so many of us had freak accidents. People like Delia, who came back because she wanted to, they're the rare ones."

The storm that killed me was unseasonable and strange. I don't want to think about it right now. If I think about it, when I'm already prisoned in glass with no way out, I may just start screaming. "So?"

"So I tried to protect you by making her think you were the anchor, so she wouldn't make a replacement. You're the one who's always saying we have an obligation to other people. To help them."

I stare at him. I don't know if he can see me; I hope he can. I hope he understands the hate and dismay I'm directing at his face. "She knew I wasn't the anchor; she said as much to me. I was trying to convince you to volunteer at the suicide hotline, not giving you permission to lock other ghosts in mirrors so rich assholes can use us as the fountain of youth. This isn't helping people."

"Getting old doesn't help them either."

"Getting old is *natural*. It's what we didn't get. Every time I take a call, I am fighting to help someone else get old. This is sick. It's wrong, and you need to let me out of here."

"That's not going to happen. I could maybe convince Teresa not to sell you right away. If you wanted to stay.

We could talk more about why this is okay. Why this is how things ought to be. If you wanted."

I'm so tired. "Go to hell, Danny," I say, and he looks surprised for a moment before he puts the mirror down and disappears.

I start to pace. I'm trapped in glass. I'm going to be exploited and held prisoner forever, like an unwilling genie in a breakable bottle. The old stories said you needed to cover all the mirrors after someone died so that they wouldn't prison your ghosts. They also said the first person who looked at their reflection after a ghost *did* get caught would drop dead on the spot, frightened out of themselves, but Teresa looked at me, and she lived. Is it because she's a witch? Are witches immune to that sort of terror? Is it because she's the one who prisoned me there? Or is there something else I ought to know, something I'm missing because this has never happened to me before?

One ghost to a mirror. Can't share your prison. And people who look in mirrors containing the dead sometimes die for no apparent reason, like they weren't able to stand what they saw. Ghosts can move time. What if that's not all that we can do?

Trouble with being a teenage runaway is no one tells you anything. Most people grow out of it, though; start making connections, start making allies, start making *friends.* Forty years I've been running, and I can count the friends I've made on the fingers of one hand. They're bright, precious things, every one of them, but they're not enough. They didn't tell me the things I needed to know. Forty years in the ground, and I'm still lost when it comes to the realities of what I am.

In a world of anchors and moorings, I am a nail in someone else's coffin, and no one can tell who's been buried beneath me.

I stop, take a breath I don't need, and try to center myself. It's not as easy as it would be if I had eyelids I could close or hands I could see, but I've had a long time to grow accustomed to the troubles of this world. Sometimes my body is solid and seems alive. Sometimes it passes through walls. Right now, it might as well be missing altogether. It's all the same. I endure. I last. I am Jenna Pace, I am no longer Jenna-who-runs, and I will find my way out of this.

I don't know how long I wait, a snake poised to strike, for my mirror to be uncovered. The world shifts subtly around me. I don't know what that means, whether the mirror is being moved or whether mirror-landscapes just move sometimes, but I keep my place and my peace, and I wait as patiently as I can. Anything else would mean giving up, and that's the one thing I can't do. Patty wouldn't want things to end this way.

I've been fighting to earn my way back to my sister for so long. I refuse to let this be what stops me.

When the mirror is finally uncovered, the shift is sudden enough to be jarring. One moment, the world is gilded silver, unbroken and unyielding, and the next, one entire wall of my existence has been replaced with a face I've never seen before, a man with wrinkles in the skin around his hope-filled eyes and a tight, miserly set to his sunken mouth. There are calculations scored into his skin like hooks, numbers I can almost see in the way he is assessing me. This man can see me.

"A ghost under glass?" he says. "That's your miracle solution? How did you—"

If I am to do this, I must do it. I've never killed anyone before. I've saved so many lives, but I've never killed. Maybe the scales will balance. Maybe there's a cosmic score sheet somewhere, and it will show that I am still a good girl. Maybe I don't care. I will not end my existence under someone else's glass.

Without thinking, without feeling, I move. I flow out of the silver and into the dusty blue of this stranger's eyes, the mirrors he uses to see the world. I don't see him as he stiffens, but I feel it, feel his heart start and stutter in his chest, feel it fall out of synch with itself. If I was going to let him go, this would be the moment to do it. I can't, I can't. I still feel the mirror pulling on me, trying to drag me back into its borders. If I let go of the man who has become my anchor to the real world, I'll be pulled back into the silver in an instant, and I don't think I can do this again. It *hurts*. The silver clings to the outline of what should be my skin, burning and blistering me.

The first one who looks will die, I think, and that's what the stories always said: that the mirror had to be covered until the ghosts had gone, or the *first* person who looked would feel their heart stop in their chest, would feel the world ripped away and shredded into nothingness. Not the second, not the last; only the first. Witches don't count, or I wouldn't be able to move, but still. This is not something I can do again.

The world has always had rules. The trick is finding them.

I am not possessing him, this cruel-lipped man who picked up my mirror and looked at me like I was the answer to a question he'd almost given up on asking. I am . . . *inhabiting* him, shoving myself into the space between the intake of breath and the beating of the heart. His breath hitches in his chest one more time before he collapses, crumpling to the floor like so much discarded meat. The silver tether snaps as the mirror drops from his hand and shatters, smooth glass becoming powder on the concrete floor of the alley behind the theater.

I am free.

Substance comes back to me in an instant, my feet hitting the ground a split second after the mirror, standing over the fallen body of the old man who would have used me to make himself young again. I turn, and there she is, the new witch with Brenda's eyes. Teresa. That's what Danny called her.

She stares at me, eyes wide and frightened. Then they narrow, fear giving way to rage.

"You little poltergeist," she spits. "Do you know what you've done? That was Jack Bandy. He was the oldest water witch this side of the Mississippi. He has allies you can't even imagine, and you've killed him. They'll end you."

"First person looks in a mirror, their heart will stop. If he was a witch, guess you didn't count because you put me there." I step away from the body, cooling meat that *I* made, corpse that I put into the world. My eyes remain on Teresa. I can't trust her not to have another mirror ready and waiting. Woman like this, when she goes to war against the world, she does it with all the tools she thinks she's going to need. "Where's your mama? She probably has a few things to say about this whole thing. Don't think she's going to be too happy with your part in it."

My accent is coming back, stronger than it's been in decades. I sound like the Hollow, and not like the washed-out memory of the South I've been since I left. I'm glad of that much. If this is where I end—if this alley is where I get locked in glass forever—I may as well go knowing that I sound like home.

Some of the fear comes back into Teresa's eyes. "She's not here."

"She was in the theater with me when you took me. You a corn witch like she is? I know your daddy was, so I guess if those things run in families, it would make sense for you to carry the same seeds in your soul. Corn witches big on prisoning ghosts in glass? I thought your people would have raised you better."

She takes a step toward me, hand raised to the level of her shoulder, and the world shifts around us. She's a corn witch like her parents: I can hear the rustle of leaves in the distance as the field responds to her anger. Corn can break concrete, if it grows fast enough. I'm not sure corn can *hurt* me, but if anyone can teach me otherwise, it's probably her.

"Don't you talk about my people, dead girl," she spits. "You think you have some sort of rights here? You just killed a man. Dead things shouldn't be killers. That's not how the world works."

"I died because the world isn't always nice; doesn't make me any less of a person," I say, and my words are as true today as they were forty years ago, when I ran out into a storm and the sky fell down on my head. "You locked me up. I let me out. What were you *thinking*?"

"That nothing happens by mistake," she says. We're both stalling. She's trying to call the corn; I'm trying to figure out what comes next. As long as we're in this holding pattern, I can wait to see what happens. "Ghosts can grant life. You think God did that by accident? You're tools for the living, and you're *selfish*. You don't let go. You don't give what you've got."

"We're not tools," I say. "We're as human as you are. Witches can do things too, but I don't see many of you standing up and offering to serve the whole of humanity."

"They'd use us."

"You'd use me."

Silence falls, uncomfortable and tight, heavy with the weight of everything that hasn't yet been said.

Then the corn bursts through the ground.

It's growing faster than summer kudzu, grabbing for my ankles like rustling hands. Teresa's eyes are filled with fury, her hand spread wide as she beckons the spreading field onward. I don't think, don't pause, just move: I leap for the nearest wall, letting go of solidity in the moment before impact. I pass through the brick, and the alley falls away, leaving me temporarily alone, with no idea what's coming next.

13

Mama, Mama, Make My Bed

I need to find Brenda. She must know by now that it's her daughter we're up against: two corn witches can't possibly be this close together without noticing each other. I know she said witches don't feel each other the way that ghosts do, but they're using the same thing as a focus for their magic. Surely the corn will tell them, if nothing else does.

Ghosts always know when there's another ghost around. We change the way the air feels. It's the change I notice first, before Danny reaches through the wall on the other side of me, grabs my hair, and drags me into the dark of the auditorium beyond.

He's insubstantial, but so am I; there are no barriers to his hands finding what little substance I have, no rules that forbid his fingers to close around my throat. He can't strangle me—I don't need air under the best of circumstances, and certainly not when I'm essentially air myself—but old habits die hard, and so he squeezes and I flail, until I manage to break his grip and shove myself away.

He glares at me, and when he opens his mouth, there is no sound, but I understand him all the same. Ghosts can always speak to ghosts, even when the rest of the world would dismiss us as nothing but wind and shadows.

Why couldn't you stay in New York? he demands. *Why couldn't you stay away, and let me have this?*

You're hurting people, I reply. *You're helping a witch against your own kind.*

Danny says nothing, because there's nothing for Danny to say. He sold us out for the promise of peace and being left alone. I wish I could say I don't understand. There have been times when I'd have given anything if it meant I could keep up my little masquerade of life, keep haunting my own routines and not bothering anyone who didn't need to know what I really am. But I never hurt anyone. Not like this.

Where is she keeping the mirrors, Danny?

He doesn't answer me. I drift to where he hangs in the air, reaching out and resting the memory of my hand against the memory of his shoulder. Contact is funny when you have no skin to touch.

She's done. Brenda's not going to let her walk away from this. I hope. I pray. Can Brenda really side with the dead over her own daughter? The living are a mystery to me. I didn't spend enough time as one of them. *Show me where the mirrors are, and maybe I won't tell Brenda where to find you.*

He turns his face away. I wait.

Finally, soundlessly, he says, *The old supply room. She keeps them there. What are you going to do?*

I don't answer. I pull my hand away and float through the next wall, away from the man who betrayed us all, away from the distant sound of corn ripping through the alley floor. I have other things to do.

The supply room is small and dark and filled with cloth-swaddled bundles, like someone's good china. I have to solidify to begin picking them up. As the cloth falls away to reveal the mirrored surfaces beneath, the whispers of the dead begin to fill the air, soft susurrations demanding their release. I don't have to wait for them to ask me twice.

The mirrors shatter when I drop them, scattering silver glitter across the floor. As each glass explodes, the ghost it contains bursts free and takes solid form, until the room is so packed that it's a good thing I don't need to breathe; there is no air here. Only bodies from wall to wall, angry, agitated, snarling bodies. They want revenge. I don't need to talk to them to know that, or to know that the only way I can keep control of this situation is to act fast. Right now, I am their savior, the one who got them out of the glass where they'd been prisoned. Give them time to realize that things have changed—that action is possible—and I'll lose them.

I grab one of the empty frames from the pile of broken mirrors and slam it against the nearest wall. The sound is big enough, sudden enough, that most of them turn to look at me. The others follow half a beat behind, unwilling to be left out of whatever's about to happen.

"This everyone?" I demand.

Muttering and whispers answer me.

"Delia's back in Manhattan playing coffin nail, and Danny's not on our side anymore, but there's more than those two in our city. So is this everyone? Count your heads, or your hands, or whatever suits you, but tell me if the breaking's done."

This time the muttering is louder, before one of the gang-girls says, "This is all of us. Where's the witch who brought us here?"

"Outside. In the corn." I glance to the wall, then back to the woman who spoke. She looks the same as she always has. Not so all of them. Some of the ghosts are older than they should be, faces seamed with new lines, hair streaked with new runnels of gray. "How much time did she have you bleed?"

The mutters contain numbers this time. Years: she

bled off years, some her own, some belonging to other people. This was the use she saw for us, prisoned under glass and giving youth back to those who don't deserve it, all while forbidding us to move on. My heart hardens a little more. That's good. It'll need to be hard for what's to come.

Some things are anathema to softness.

"She's a corn witch," I say. "The soil listens when she speaks. Her ma's here, and Mill Hollow answers best to family. We need to keep her distracted long enough for Brenda to come and bring things to a finish. Then we can go home. Back to Manhattan. Back to our dailies." Because we don't have lives, not really; we're the long-dead, the cold, and the lost. But we still have our daily routines, the steps we go through, the things we choose to do. Those are the things we all want to return to.

"How?" asks a hollow-eyed man in a grocer's apron.

I smile. I shrug, spreading my empty hands wide.

"I have no idea," I say. "But we start by going through that wall."

I point. They follow my hand, and when I let go of solidity and drift through the brick, they follow *me*.

We flow through the wall like a river of ectoplasm and rage, surrounding Teresa, sliding through the corn, even as the leaves slash at the substance of our skins. She shrieks, furious and impotent, and we swirl around her, untouched and untouchable. She would kill us, if we weren't already dead. She would prison us back under glass, if all her mirrors weren't broken, ground down to dust and rendered useless by our escape. The same mirror can't catch two ghosts, and with all the fragments mixed and mingled on the floor, all mirrors are the same mirror. Her only weapon is her life, which is so precious, and so temporary.

Her shrieks turn pained when the first ghost brushes against her skin and forces the years she gave them back into her body. She smacks them away, hair lightening and skin loosening as I watch. There are too many of us and only one of her. We could weaken her an inch at a time, a death of a thousand cuts and a million stolen moments. What happens to a living body aged past its natural dying day by the dead? Will she collapse, or will we turn her aged and immortal, unable to let go, unable to move on?

I don't know. I don't know, and I don't *want* to know. "*Stop!*" I yell, and my voice is wind and agony, and there is nothing I can do, nothing I can do to stop them, nothing I can do to save her.

"Stop," says another voice, softer than mine, older than mine, wearier than mine. I turn, and there's Brenda, her guitar over her back as it always is, her eyes hidden in the shadow. The ghosts stop moving. So does the corn. Teresa's struggles no longer stir it; it hangs, frozen as a knife on the verge of dropping, as the world waits to see what will follow.

"Terry, girl, I thought we taught you better," says Brenda. The weariness deepens as she wades into the green, brushing ghosts aside like we were cobwebs. We were drawn into a fight bigger and wilder than we are, and I find I can't even be angry that the end of it isn't mine. We'll survive. That's all the victory I need.

"Corn's not enough anymore," says Teresa. There's a little fire in her words. Of course the corn isn't enough. It never could have been.

"It'll have to be," says Brenda. She takes her daughter's chin between her thumb and forefinger, studying the younger woman's eyes before she leans in and presses a kiss against her forehead. "From now on, it'll have to be."

The change is so swift and so inevitable that for a moment, I don't see what's happening. Their skin roughens, ripples; their clothes grow green with husks. Still together, still touching, they burst into cornstalks and continue to rush upward, until they tower over us, until the field is spreading out to claim the theater, pulling it down one brick at a time. Brenda's guitar falls. I rush to catch it, becoming substantial and grabbing it by the neck before it can hit the ground.

By the time the ghosts and I reach the street, the theater is gone. Only the corn remains. There is no sign of

Danny. Maybe it's better that way.

"How are we getting home?" asks a ghost.

"Anyone know how to drive?" I reply, and laugh, filling my lungs with Mill Hollow air, watching the cornfield spread all the way to the ravine. A few people will be mighty surprised when they wake up in the morning. Or maybe not. It's hard to say, in a place like this one, on a night when the moon is like a panther's eye and the corn stretches out to the end of the world.

14

Make It Up Both Long and Narrow

A couple of the ghosts knew how to drive. It's been five days, and we're all home, and the world is exactly like it's always been, and the world is totally new.

Delia and Avo were glad to have me back. The cats didn't really notice. Delia has been in and out of my apartment since that night, feeding them, learning their little ways. She never asked if it was all right with me, and I'm grateful for that. She's been around a long time. I think she has her ways of knowing things.

I think she might have known before I did.

It's almost midnight, and I've been walking for hours, following the alleys, following the rustle of little rat feet on the concrete. It's almost anticlimactic when I come around a bend and there she is, Sophie, tucked down between two trash cans with a nest of ratlings in her lap. She looks up at the sound of my footsteps. She relaxes when she sees who they belong to.

"Jenna," she says. Her gaze sharpens, becoming puzzled, then sad. "That's Brenda's guitar."

"Brenda had to go." I offer the guitar to her. She takes it reverently, glancing at me to be sure it's all right, that I truly mean it, that this isn't some cruel joke. "I thought you might like this."

"Yes, yes; thank you, yes," she says. Then she frowns. "Did you want something in return?"

"I'd like to ask for something. It's on you whether you give it."

"What do you want?"

I take a breath. Am I really ready for this? I could stop now. I could wait a little longer. There's always more time, if you're willing to take it. That's one of the beautiful things about being outside the normal flow of things. It's easy to see that there's *always* more time.

But I'm tired. I've gone home and I've seen that there's nothing left to run from, and I'm done. This is right. This is how it finishes.

"I've earned it," I say softly. "I've earned my last day. I want to take it from you."

Sophie's eyes widen. Then, wordlessly, she nods, and offers me her hand. Her fingers are smaller than mine, delicate and soft; it's like holding hands with a child. The time flows out of her and into me, and I am a day older, I am a day closer to the grave, and there it is, finally, finally, after all this time, after all this running;

I've reached the border of my dying day.

Sophie's eyes widen further still, until I have to wonder what she's seeing when she looks at me. Something has changed for her; I know that much. Something has changed for both of us.

"There you are."

I turn and there's Patty standing in the alley behind me, a smile on her face and a plastic flower barrette in her hair. I don't think. I just run, yanking my hand away from Sophie and throwing my arms around my sister, burying my face against her skin. She smells of salt and peppermint soap. She caresses my hair, and everything is all right. Everything is going to be just fine.

"Took you long enough."

I lift my head to look at her. The alley is gone. Sophie is gone. I'm a little sorry about that. I'd been meaning to say goodbye.

"Have you been waiting all this time?"

Patty shrugs, like it makes no difference to her; like forty years was the blink of an eye. "Not *all* this time. I had to show Ma and Pa where to go. Now I get to walk with you. All the way home."

"You won't leave me again, will you?"

"Never." Patty's hand slips into mine and holds me, holds me fast, the two Pace girls against the weight and width of the world. When she turns, I turn with her, and we walk, side by side, into the silvery light of something more than a mirror, something less than a moon. I don't know where we're going, but I know this:

It's been a lot of years and a lot of miles, but I'm finally going home. And I am not afraid.

About the Author

Photograph by Beckett Gladney

SEANAN MCGUIRE is the author of the October Daye urban fantasy series, the InCryptid series, and several other works, both stand-alone and in trilogies. She also writes darker fiction as Mira Grant.

Seanan lives in a creaky old farmhouse in Northern California, which she shares with her cats, a vast collection of creepy dolls and horror movies, and sufficient books to qualify her as a fire hazard.

She was the winner of the 2010 John W. Campbell Award for Best New Writer, and in 2013 she became the first person ever to appear five times on the same Hugo ballot.

TOR·COM

**Science fiction. Fantasy. The universe.
And related subjects.**

*

More than just a publisher's website, *Tor.com*
is a venue for **original fiction, comics,** and
discussion of the entire field of SF and fantasy,
in all media and from all sources. Visit our site
today—and join the conversation yourself.